Sleepless Nights Complete Collection Of Thriller Stories

D.S. Bankert

Published by D.S. Bankert, 2024.

SLEEPLESS NIGHTS COMPLETE COLLECTION OF THRILLER STORIES

First edition. August 25, 2024.

Copyright © 2024 D.S. Bankert.

ISBN: 979-8227878830

Written by D.S. Bankert.

Cemetery Gate Keys

In 1978, in a small town in Maine, two teenaged boys disappeared without a trace. Police only found a stained piece of shirt and old cemetery keys.

On July 21st, 1978, Robert and James went for a walk. As the two boys started to pass a wooded area, they saw an old, partially covered trail. Robert said to James they should take the old trail and see where it takes them. James followed Robert down the trail. The teens had to remove the overgrowth of vines and brush.

As the boy's ventured deeper down the trail, they noticed a foul smell coming from somewhere. They soon found where the foul smell was coming from. Alongside the old trail were rotting rodents that had been decaying. The two keep walking down the path as Robert stepped on something sticking out of the dirt. Robert bent down and removed the item. It was a set of old cemetery keys on a large ring. One key was larger than the other two keys. It was a skeleton key.

The teens walked what felt like miles down the trail. James suddenly stopped and just pointed down the path. Robert looked at what James was pointing at. It were small bones scattered across the trail. James was afraid and shaking. Robert told James it was only bones from an old animal that had died and nothing more. James ran past the scattered bones as Robert followed. The boy's saw the trail opening ahead.

As Robert and James saw the trail opening to a larger area, they suddenly stopped, it was an old cemetery. The cemetery had a wrought iron fence going around it. The size of the cemetery was huge. The boy's stood in front of a large arched wrought iron gate.

Robert went to use the cemetery keys he found. He tried the first key, it did not open the gate. Robert then tried the larger skeleton key, the gate unlocked. The boy's walked through the large gate's opening. "Robert gasped" it was rows and rows of Mausoleums. They walked around the cemetery, looking at the old headstones. They could not see the deceased person's name on the headstone, but only the date of 1896.

Robert went to one of the mausoleum doors. He used the skeleton key to enter the crypt. As the two entered the mausoleum, the heavy stench of mold was in the air. Suddenly, the door slammed shut behind them. We locked ourselves in now!! James screamed! Robert slammed the door with his body. The heavy door would not budge.

As the two teens panicked to get out. James saw a small opening at the base of the mausoleum. Robert started to crawl through the narrow opening as James followed him. It was a dug out tunnel. The tunnel was narrow and long. The boy's finally came to the end of the tunnel. A small door with a lock on it was directly in front of them.

Robert took out the keys and tried to unlock the small door. The skeleton key was too large for the lock. He then used the smaller key and the door unlocked. As the two boys entered the old house, the smell of decay was thick. The dug out tunnel opened to a large room.

Sheets covered the furniture in the room. As they crawled on top of the furniture, people could see spiders. As the boy's walked around, James stepped on a letter. He picked up the letter and dropped it to the floor. Maine Mortuary Services received the letter. Bloodstains covered it. Then Robert realized that people used this house as a mortuary. The two keep looking around the house. James walked over to a partially open door. They descended the stairs into the cellar. The cellar door slammed shut.

Robert ran to the top of the stairs with James and tried to force the cellar door back open. A large wood piece must have fallen and blocked the door. The only way to find a way out now was to go into the cellar.

To look for another way out. They began to descend the staircase into the cellar. The cellar floor was scattered with old stone caskets. As the boy's started to travel through the maze of casket's they heard a loud moan.

As the two boys heard a loud moan come from the cellar. They saw a large shadow figure form in the corner of the cellar. Robert and James ran to a nearby door. Wood blocked the door. As Robert frantically started to remove the wood away from the door. James just stared at the shadow figure moving slowly toward them.

Just as Robert removed the last piece of wood away from the door, the shadow figure darted toward them. The teens ran in and slammed the door shut and locked it with the keys. As they ascended the stairs to the upper room. A shadow figure transferred through the locked door. Robert and James ran to the upper room and barricaded the door with furniture from the room.

James ran to a window in the room and opened it. All James could see was the moonlight against the outside bars covering the window. Then, he realized that they were trapped.

A load growl came from the cellar. As James looked out of a small crack in the large wooden door. He gasped as a creature with glowing, bright orange eyes was coming up the stairway toward the door. The creature smashed the door in.

The creature stopped and stared at James and Robert. Blood was dripping out of its mouth. The hair on the creature was matted down and smelled putrid. The creature then attacked Robert, first slashing him with its powerful claws. Robert fell to the floor dead as James ran to a small closet in the room.

The creature looked confused. James covered his mouth. The creature started to pass the closet and suddenly stopped. James stood silent as he gazed upon the creature's glowing orange eyes. The sight of the bright glowing orange eyes will be eternally etched in James' memory. All of a sudden, the creature burst open the closet door and attacked James with its sharp claws. As James started to lose consciousness, sliding to the floor. The creature made a loud growl as it devoured James.

No one has ever seen the two boys again. The townspeople believe the cemetery has a curse. Any person who enters the cemetery will never return. The days turned into months after the two teens went missing. The entire town helped in the search for the two boys. Some townspeople recall last seeing Robert and James walking toward the old trail.

Five years after the boy's disappearance, three girls walked by the old trail. The eldest girl, Robin, said hey girls, that is the old trail the townspeople always say stay away from. Let's go down the trail. As the girls walked down the trail, they heard some townspeople yelling for them to not go down the old trail. The girls have never been seen again. The police roped off the old trail in hopes that no one else would ever go into the woods again. As the police walked the trail deep in the woods, they found parts of the trail soaked in blood. They had not found any bodies, only a girl's watch and one shoe.

The Lighthouse on Bloodstained Rock

There is an old lighthouse far north called the lighthouse on bloodstained rock. The lighthouse earned its name because people carried out horrific deaths there. Prisoners and accused people died in horrifying and terrifying ways. If the prisoner was lucky, they took them outside and shot them. Torturers had tortured and killed most prisoners. The guards chained the prisoner to the stone lighthouse during low tide. As the tide rose, the prisoner drowned.

Because of the haunted lighthouse, people avoid going near the rocks that lead to it. In the spring of 1987, a woman stayed at the lighthouse. During that time, the lighthouse discovered several bodies floating away. The police would speak to the lighthouse keeper. They wanted to know if she heard or knew anything about the bodies. Searchers discovered the bodies floating downstream from the lighthouse. She stated she knew nothing about the poor soles that had lost their lives.

The police found new bloodstains on the rocks at the lighthouse. They also found a broken wooden boat. The keeper told the police she didn't know. Maybe the men were drunk and misjudged the distance to the lighthouse. They crashed the boat into the rocks. I heard nothing whatsoever. The police were leaving the lighthouse when the keeper saw a boat approaching. When the men entered her lighthouse, she had a strange smile, like she was planning something. As the day became evening, the keeper saw the boat's lights coming towards her lighthouse. The lights were yellow and orange, and she saw them through the windows. The men reached the lighthouse. The keeper stood on the bloodstained rock platform. The keeper yelled out good evening gentlemen, please dock your boat here. You are more than welcome to lodge here for the night.

As the men stared at the keeper, they could not see her whole face, only one part of a slight smile. The men went into the old lighthouse. The keeper heard them talk about a bad smell in the walls. I have just made some food, your men must be hungry after your journey. Please sit and will shall eat. Because people believe that this old lighthouse is haunted, I am unable to dine with them. As the men ate the food the keeper gave them, one man noticed the keeper's bowl of food had not been touched. He said, hey keeper, why have you not eaten your food yet. The keeper began to laugh loudly and said I always let the gentleman eat first. As soon as she completed her statement, some men began to feel ill. One man tried to stop the other men from eating the food, it was too late. One man shouted, she has poisoned us.

Why have you done this to us, you horribly witch? The keeper reached over and grabbed a large knife and began to slowly walk from one ill man to another. She stabbed a man and held a cup under the wound to catch the blood. The other men were too weak to do anything. They watched in horror as the woman drained their blood in a satanic ritualistic way. The last man could speak, please why did you do this? I have to keep the lighthouse rocks blood coated to appease the spirits that met their fate here. They promised me they would not harm me as long as I used the blood to cover the rocks. You are the last lucky man, you are the ultimate sacrifice. I will drag you outside and spill your blood directly on the rock to make the spirits of this place happy. As the keeper grabbed the man by the feet and dragged him outside to sacrifice him on the rocks.

The keeper stopped as she heard a loud bang behind her. As the keeper turned to look behind her, a tall man stepped out of the darkness with his gun pointing at the keeper. Drop the knife or I will shoot you. The keeper yelled out, you have lived here as long as I have and know what I have to do to appease the spirits. As she raised the knife, the tall man shot the keeper in the head as she fell to the stone. The man said, Oh, may god thank you for saving me from this witch. The tall man began to laugh, I did not do this to help you. I did this to become the new lighthouse keeper. The man reached into his pocket and opened a knife. As he began stabbing the man, he said he was sorry, but the spirits of the rock need the blood.

The Total Extraction

Thomas Smith was a 21-year-old male that lived in a small town in Texas his whole life. He worked at a local grocery store part-time while attending school. The community knew Thomas very well. People considered Thomas to be a polite young man. He started to have some problems with his teeth. Thomas knew he had to go to the towns' dentist. The towns' dentist made him extremely uneasy. Thomas decided to go to the dentist after school. As Thomas walked to the local dentist, he notices a black truck parked behind the dentist's office.

As Thomas walked into the dentist's office, he noticed the front desk secretary crying. Thomas said to her, are you ok? She stated to Thomas she was ok and sorry she was crying. She asked Thomas to sign in, and the dentist would be with him shortly. As Thomas was signing in, he heard a loud bang and the dentist came out of a room with blood all over his hands. Thomas gasped as the look on the dentists face looked very upset. Thomas got up and started to leave as the secretary said, wait Thomas, the dentist is ready for you now. He stopped with a slightly concerned look on his face. He turned and entered the room as the dentist entered the room. Hi Thomas, good to see you, stated the dentist. You always had my perfect teeth.

Thomas asked the dentist a question. I did not see anyone leave this room before I entered it. The dentist sometimes said they leave through the back door. When the dentist spoke, two men quickly placed a big bag into the black truck behind the office. Thomas said, what are those two men doing behind your dentist's office? The dentist said, don't worry about that, Thomas. I am going to give you a shot in your mouth now. I love your teeth so much, Thomas. Thomas said to the dentist, he changed his mind. The dentist said to Thomas, you really think I can let you leave now after asking about the two men. Thomas pushed the dentist away and ran out of the office.

As Thomas ran, he saw the dentist running with the two men behind him. The dentist screamed, Thomas, I will get my teeth from you. Thomas ran home and told his parents about what had happened at the dentist's office. Oh, Thomas! The dentist is just old and somewhat strange, stated his father. Thomas decided to sneak out and investigate behind the dentist office. Thomas walked to the dentist's office. He looked into the window and saw two men eating with the dentist. He walked behind the dentist's office and walked toward the black truck. Thomas opened the unlocked truck door and climbed inside. He saw several bags in the back. As he opened the first bag, he screamed. The head of a person was in the bag covered with blood and their mouth was open with all teeth pulled.

As he jumped out of the truck, the two men ran toward him as he ran past them. The two men grabbed him as he screamed. The men brought him to the dentist's office. The dentist was getting ready to give Thomas a shot. As he moved closer to Thomas, the dentist yelled, what did you do, Thomas. Thomas started laughing as the dentist tried to move away, he saw a large syringe sticking out of his leg. Why did you do that? I injected you with my solution first. What solution, paint thinner, Thomas yelled. The dentist dropped the syringe as Thomas kicked the men holding him. Thomas ran out of the office yelling I have my perfect teeth, and you have a slow death.

The Haunted Boathouse

In the fall of 1998, a young married couple bought a small home of their dreams located in Bangor, Maine. The home was on the water and with a boat house. The couple adored the Victorian style of the home, which was built in 1912. Jason was a handy man who worked on boats. His wife Audrey was a stay at home mother. The couple's daughters, Jamie, was 8 and Kim was 10. The two girls loved living on the water.

One early morning, Jamie woke up to a loud bang outside as she peered out of the window toward the old boathouse. Jamie stood in shock as she saw an older man walking slowly toward the old boathouse. The older man turned slowly and looked toward the house. Jamie quickly ducked below the window to avoid the man seeing him. She raised her head slowly to check if the old man saw her. When she saw him staring at her below the window, she screamed. Jason ran into the room Jamie what is wrong with you why are you screaming. She pointed outside there was an old man in our yard, he was walking toward the boathouse. Jason ran outside and walked toward the old boathouse. No one was outside as Jason walked around the property to see if anyone was outside.

The following day, Jason was outside working on the yard when he heard a woman speaking softly. She asked who he was and why he was in their house. As Jason looked toward the boathouse, he saw a glimpse of a woman in the window of the boathouse. Once again, Jason heard the soft voice as he walked into the boathouse. You need to search beneath the boathouse. Jason ran to the house for a flashlight to look into the darker water in the boathouse.

Jason went back to the boathouse. He saw a woman pointing into the dark water. Once someone noticed her, she disappeared. Jason turned on the flashlight as he searched the dark water. A glimmer of something shining as the light hit an object under the water. Jason accidentally dropped the flashlight into the dark water. He jumped into the dark water and saw a big stone covered in silt. There was a chain attached to it. Using his hands, he cleared the silt and was shocked to discover a skeleton. It wrapped the chain around its leg. Jason blacked out and started to sink quickly into the dark water below him.

Audrey quickly jumped into the water and brought Jason to the surface. As she pushed on his stomach, he began to cough up water. Jason was ok as his wife had Jamie run to get her father a blanket. Jason walked slowly to the house with his family as he told Audrey what he had just seen. Audrey listened to Jason's story as she called the police. The police came and sent divers into the dark water to retrieve the body. The divers resurfaced, and the couple was shocked.

The divers retrieved multiple bodies from the water. Jason said to Audrey, Oh my god Audrey, what has happened here. Audrey looked at Kim shaking and staring at Jason. Kim, why are you shaking, stated Audrey. Mom, I saw dad walking to the boathouse late at night as a woman followed him into the old boat house. I was too afraid to tell you I had never seen the woman before. When the police asked Jason about the woman, divers found her belongings in a small purse.

As the officer opened the purse and looked at the ID of the woman, he gasped. This is the woman who has been missing for many days. When the police looked at Jason, he had a confused expression. Then, he started laughing and confessed that he killed the woman. He claimed that a woman with a gentle voice told him to do it. The police took Jason into custody. As the officer looked back toward the old boathouse, he saw a woman in the window of the boathouse looking out. Many weeks later, Audrey put the house up for sale, hoping to move away and have a new start for her and her daughters. As she walked to the back of her house toward the old boathouse, she saw a woman's face in the window of the old boathouse. She stood in fear as she realized Jason actually did see a woman inside the boathouse. Audrey walked slowly toward the old boathouse as the image of the woman's face disappeared.

As she entered the boat house, she heard a soft voice speak to her. Jason brought many women to the boathouse. He killed them and hid their bodies. The voice seemed grateful. The uncovering of the secret brought relief and peace to the departed. Audrey walked out of the boathouse and entered the front of the house. A car passing by pulled in her driveway and asked Audrey how much she was selling her house for. Audrey stated to the driver, I am sorry I have changed my mind. I will not be selling my house at this point. Audrey and her daughters lived in the old-fashioned house for a long time. They never saw a ghost again.

Deep Into The Eerie Dark Woods

Eric and Thomas, two teens from Virginia, plan to hike the Appalachian Mountains for a while. The trails in the dark woods area have a slight haze due to the rain and humidity. The two made sure they brought enough gear to make their journey. The rain flowed through the plants on the mountain, making a soft sound. The teens felt a slight cooling effect and welcomed the calm, cool air. Eric yelled back to Thomas once they come to the small stream ahead, they can stop and take a break for a while.

The two started to unpack some of their food to eat, such as dried fruit, water and prepackaged meals. As the two ate their meals, the daylight started to diminish and turned to dusk. Thomas said to Eric they should set up camp before dark. Eric agreed that was a good idea. Thomas began unpacking his tent when they heard a loud crack from above on the mountain ledge. The two decided to ignore the sound from above them and continue to set up their camp. Eric decided to start a small fire for the evening. The bright, luminous glow of the fire shined on the teens faces as they began to fall asleep.

Suddenly, a deafening crash happened in front of the two as they sat in front of the fire. Eric jumped up and looked toward Thomas as he saw something large run into the dark woods. Oh my god, Thomas, what the hell was that. Thomas screamed what happened. Eric said, as I jumped up, I just saw a huge animal run behind you into the dark woods. Thomas said, stop playing with me.

Eric said No, I saw something run past you and I don't know what it was. The two grabbed a flashlight and Eric screamed. The flashlight hit a bloody deer head nearby. Oh my god, Thomas, we have to get out of here. No, Eric, we have to stay here until daylight, we don't know our way out of here in the dark. Eric, we have our knives and a handgun, remember.

We can stay up in shifts to keep guard over one another until daylight, ok. Eric replied that he felt scared, but he would take the first shift guarding with the handgun. Thomas loaded the small handgun and gave it to Eric while he tried to get some sleep. As Thomas slept, Eric began to become tired. Then he heard a crackling sound coming from behind them. He pointed his flashlight into the woods. In the distance, he saw glowing eyes looking at him.

As Eric heard another sound in front of him, he aimed the handgun at the glowing eyes. As Eric looked in front of him, he saw another set of glowing eyes in the distance, slowly moving closer to their camp. Suddenly, Eric saw an animal with glowing eyes running toward him, he aimed his gun and shot. Thomas jumped up as Eric screamed and ran out of the tent to find Eric. He saw the flashlight laying on the ground and quickly grabbed it. Shining the flashlight into the dark woods, he saw something hanging low it the tree line.

Thomas was shocked when he saw something hanging in the trees. He covered his mouth in horror. It was a bloody piece of Eric's clothing. He began to scream for Eric, with no response back. Thomas ran back to his tent and zippered it shut as he began to grab his knife. Thomas sat in the tent, trembling. He hoped the thing in the dark woods would leave, so he could search for Eric in the morning. He started to hear a slight crackling sound outside his tent.

Suddenly, a slight shadow appeared on the side of the tent. The shadow was cast be an animal, huge and right outside the tent. Thomas grasped his knife as he prayed the large animal would leave him alone. The creature made a loud screech as it ran into the woods. Thomas stayed awake all night until daylight came. He opened his tent and very slowly stepped outside. As he approached the smoldering fire, he saw blood laying on the ground next to the chair Eric was sitting on. The handgun was laying on the ground covered with blood. Thomas looked around and could not see any trace of Eric.

Thomas packed his camp up and began his hike back to their car. As he walked slowly through the dense woods, he saw drops of blood along the trail. He walked what seemed to be miles until he saw something on the path way in front of him. As he approached it, he started screaming, it was Eric's arm mangled and covered with bugs. Thomas started running as fast as he could down the trail.

He heard something behind him. He looked back and saw a big animal running towards him quickly. Thomas suddenly stopped. He knew he couldn't outrun the creature. He took aim as it darted toward him. Thomas shot at the creature. It looked as if it got hit by the bullets. The creature ran into the woods and stopped chasing Thomas. Thomas continued to run down the path toward the opening to the trail.

He heard a loud scream from the creature and saw another one chasing him from far away. Thomas thought I have to make it to the Jeep. As Thomas made it to the opening to the trail and ran to the Jeep. He dropped his keys. When he leaned to grab the keys, the creature also ran into the opening to the trail. Thomas gasped as he grabbed his keys and ran to the Jeep. He opened the door and jumped into the Jeep as the creature smashed out the side window. Thomas drove off as fast as he could, and the creature's arm wedged in the side door of the Jeep. The creature screamed and blood streamed onto the Jeep's floor. Thomas drove off with the creature's severed arm stuck in the door. Thomas was never seen nor heard from again.

Stacy And The River's Edge Ghost

Stacy Adams lived in a small town in Massachusetts. She had inherited a small cottage style home from her grandmother near the river's edge. Stacy's grandmother often told her stories of seeing a ghostly woman by the river. In 1986, Stacy's grandmother, Doris, passed away at age 89 and left the small cottage to Stacy. One night, as Stacy was going to bed, she saw a ghostly figure following the river's edge away from the cottage. Oh my god, Stacy thought my grandmother was telling me the truth about the ghost.

Stacy walked to the cottage's front door. She saw the female ghost stop and look at her. The spirit started to quickly walk fast toward the cottage. Stacy slammed the door shut and dropped below the window, hoping the ghost wouldn't spot her. As she started to rise slowly to peer out of the window, she screamed as her eyes met the ghost woman's eyes. The spirit started to yell, where you have taken my son, give him back to me. Stacy spoke out, I don't have your son and I do not know where he went. As quickly as Stacy had seen the ghostly image, it disappeared without a trace.

The following day, Stacy drove into town to try to find information about the ghost woman and her child. She saw an older woman sitting on a wooden bench and walked over to speak to her. As the older woman looked at Stacy, she said to her, what do you want to know about the ghost of the river's edge. The older woman shocked Stacy when she knew what she was going to ask her. Oh my god, how did you know what I was going to ask you? Everyone who has lived in that house has asked me about the woman. The ghost woman walks endlessly up and down the river's edge in search for her son who had drowned many years back. The ghost's woman's name was Sarah, and her son's name was John. Stacy thanked the older woman for the information she provided her.

Stacy drove back to the cottage and decided to try to somehow help the ghost woman find peace. As the evening turned into night, Stacy saw the ghost woman appear along the river's edge. Stacy walked through the doorway to her cottage and walked slowly toward the ghost woman. As the spirit looked up and her eyes met Stacy's eyes, she called out, have you seen my son. Stacy told the spirit no, I am sorry your son had drowned in the river many years ago, and you must leave here now in peace.

The spirit started to scream out at Stacy, you lie about my sons' death at this river's edge. The ghost woman suddenly lunged forward toward Stacy. As Stacy ran toward the cottage, she looked back and the spirit woman was not far behind her. Stacy ran into the cottage and locked the door. As the spirit ran to the cottages' door, she began to peer into the windows as Stacy hid beneath its windows, shaking. The spirit's bright glow faded as it walked away from the cottage. Stacy thought of a plan to convince the spirit her son had drowned in the river.

The next day, Stacy looked up the drowning and found a photo of the drowned young boy. Stacy thought she would wait for nightfall and try to convince the spirit of her sons' death. Time slowed. Stacy saw the spirit again. It walked slowly toward the cottage. Stacy walks out of the cottage towards the ghost woman as Stacy begins to call out for her. Sarah, I have found a photo of your son. As the ghost's eyes seemed fixed on Stacy as she moved quickly towards her, Sarah called out, you have found my son.

As the spirit got close to Stacy, she dropped the photo to the ground as fear suddenly had overtaken her. Stacy began to run back to the cottage as she looked back watching Sarah reach down and pick up the photo. The spirit began to weep uncontrollably as she held the photo, she then knew her son truly did drown in the river. As the ghost woman looked at Stacy, she reached out toward Stacy as she then disappeared. The ghost woman of the river's edge was never seen again.

The Monitoring Murder Case

It seemed to be a normal Monday work day for Jason. He worked as a security officer for a well-known department store. Jason had a full-time job watching monitors for crimes in the store. As Jason began his shift at approximately 7am, he noticed something strange. The monitor suddenly went black. As Jason started to call someone for assistance, the monitor came back on. Someone not viewing his store startled Jason. As Jason looked at the monitor, it looked like a large warehouse in another country. As he began to view the monitor, he then saw two men enter his view and placed a chair in his direct view. He heard screaming and saw two men bring another man into the room. They tied him to a chair while he screamed.

Jason's expression changed quickly as he then knew the man tied to the chair was a captive prisoner of some sort. It seemed that someone had beaten the man's face badly. As the two other men came back into view, one man carried a large knife. The men asked the man tied to the chair questions, but he avoided answering by looking down. The man with the knife came into view and proceeded to start to cut off the man's fingers as he screamed. Jason closed his eyes tight as to not see the man's fate. The man's screams fell silent as Jason started to open his eyes once again.

He saw one of the men turn and look directly at the monitor recording him. He heard the man scream through the monitor. The man in the chair didn't move. There was blood on the floor. Jason reached quickly to shut the monitor down as he saw the monitor's location. Jason shut the monitor down and started to find the location quickly to call the police. As he called the police to report what he had seen. The police answered the phone and wanted to know who he was. Jason stated to them, he was afraid and wanted to report a crime he witnessed. He also explained to the police he wanted to be anonymous.

The police started to laugh at him on the phone. Jason yelled, "Why are you laughing? I want to report that someone murdered someone else." The police stated to him what you are doing now is extremely dangerous, Jason. I did not give you my name, how do you know who I am? The police told him they tracked his location. If the murderers knew where he was, they would too. Jason hung up the phone and quickly unplugged the monitors, trying to hide his location.

Jason called his supervisor and told him what had happened. His supervisor said someone called me and asked questions about you. Jason stated what did you say to them about me. Jason's supervisor Rick told Jason he said nothing to them and just hung the phone up. He told Rick that he might be in danger. The person who killed the man in the warehouse probably knows that he saw the murder and told the police.

Rick said to Jason, don't worry, I have a place you can stay and hide for a while. I do not visit this house often, I believe you will be safe there. Jason agreed to stay at the house Rick was going to let him stay at. Thank you so much, Rick. I am glad I have someone that I trust. Jason, you need to go home right away and only pack what you truly need. I will stay here and get things together for you as well. Jason took his keys and left to get his things. Rick stayed to help him. He planned to take Jason to his house for safety. They would figure out their next steps there.

As Jason entered his driveway to his house, he saw men through his windows going through the house. He started backing up slowly as to not alert the men of his presence. Jason got to the road and sped off, racing toward Ricks house. Once Jason reached Ricks house, he noticed Rick talking on his cell phone. Jason asks Rick who he was talking to, Rick replied it's no one. Let's get you out of here, Jason. I don't think we can wait any longer. Jason got into the car with Rick as the drive seemed hours and hours. Rick, where are we going, asked Jason? I have a better location Jason just in case they somehow found out where we are going.

As Jason started to dose off, they arrived at the location. We are here, Jason. I have all your things in the trunk, what you don't have I can go in town after a few days and just buy things for you. Don't worry, you will be ok. Hey Jason, I need to leave now. I will be back in just a few days. There is plenty of food and water to last you. I want to make sure no one followed us up here.

As Rick left the house, Jason watched him drive slowly down a long dirt road in the dark. Jason decided to try to eat something. He went to the refrigerator and saw some leftovers. Jason began eating, and suddenly, he heard someone talking outside. As he went to the window to look outside, he saw Ricks car and another car behind it. He heard Rick say to the men, this is not how much money you said you would pay me.

Jason could not believe what was happening, his best friend betrayed him. Suddenly, a loud bang bang rang out as Jason saw Rick fall to the ground. Jason ran to the back of the house as the men ran toward the house. Jason remembered Rick had a hand gun in the trunk of his car. As the men entered the front door, Jason dashed out of the back door, running toward Rick laying on the ground. He quickly rolled Rick over to try to find his car keys. As the men started to run out the back door of the house toward Jason, he found the keys and quickly opened the trunk. Jason grabbed the gun. He heard a loud bang. The men started shooting at him.

A bullet went through the metal trunk, narrowly missing his head. He dropped to the ground and shot at the men, hitting one in the chest. As one of the men fell to the ground, a loud voice yelled out stop, we don't have to do it this way. We can pay you money to just keep your mouth shut. Jason screamed out, just like you did to my friend Rick. Jason stood up and started shooting at the man as he ran for cover. As the man ran, someone struck him in the back. The sound of his body falling hitting the ground was deafening. Jason ran to Ricks car and fled. He was never seen again. As police came to the scene, no bodies were ever found.

Deep Into The Dark Woods

Because of the rain and humidity, the trails in the dark woods have a slight haze. Two Virginia teens named Eric and Thomas choose to hike in the Appalachian Mountains. The two made sure they brought enough gear to make their journey. The rain trickled through the plants on the mountain, cooling the air and calming the teens. Eric yelled back to Thomas once they come to the small stream ahead, they can stop and take a break for a while.

The two started to unpack some of their food to eat, such as dried fruit, water and prepackaged meals. As the two ate their meals, the daylight started to diminish and turned to dusk. Thomas said to Eric they should set up camp before dark. Eric agreed that was a good idea. Thomas began to unpack his tent when they heard a loud crack from above, higher on the mountain ledge. The two decided to ignore the sound from above them and continue to set up their camp. Eric decided to start a small fire for the evening. The bright, luminous glow of the fire shined on the teens faces as they began to fall asleep.

Suddenly, a deafening crash happened in front of the two as they sat in front of the fire. Eric jumped up and looked toward Thomas as he saw something large run into the dark woods. Oh my god, Thomas, what the hell was that. Thomas screamed what happened. Eric said, as I jumped up, I just saw a huge animal run behind you into the dark woods. Thomas said, stop playing with me.

Eric said No, I saw something run past you and I don't know what it was. The two grabbed a flashlight. They wanted to look around. But then Eric screamed. The flashlight had hit a deer head covered in blood. It was on the ground. It was close to where they had been sitting. Oh my god, Thomas, we have to get out of here. No, Eric, we have to stay here until daylight, we don't know our way out of here in the dark. Eric, we have our knives and a handgun, remember.

We can stay up in shifts to keep guard over one another until daylight, ok. Eric replied that he felt scared, but he would take the first shift guarding with the handgun. Thomas loaded the small handgun and gave it to Eric while he tried to get some sleep. As Thomas slept, Eric began to become tired. Then he heard a crackling sound coming from behind them. He used his flashlight to look into the dark woods. He saw glowing eyes far away.

Eric aimed the gun at the glowing eyes. He heard another sound from in front of him. As Eric looked in front of him, he saw another set of glowing eyes in the distance, slowly moving closer to their camp. Suddenly, Eric saw an animal with glowing eyes running toward him, he aimed his gun and shot. Thomas jumped up as Eric screamed and ran out of the tent to find Eric. He saw the flashlight laying on the ground and quickly grabbed it. Shining the flashlight into the dark woods, he saw something hanging low it the tree line.

Thomas hurriedly approached the trees, curious about what hung from their branches. Suddenly, his eyes widened and he covered his mouth in shock. It was a blood-stained garment that belonged to Eric. He began to scream for Eric, with no response back. Thomas ran back to his tent and zippered it shut as he began to grab his knife. Thomas sat in the tent, trembling. He hoped whatever lurked in the dark woods would leave, so he could search for Eric in the light of day. He started to hear a slight crackling sound outside his tent. Suddenly, a slight shadow appeared on the side of the tent. The shadow was cast be an animal, huge and right outside the tent.

Thomas grasped his knife as he prayed the large animal would leave him alone. The creature made a loud screech as it ran into the woods. Thomas stayed awake all night until daylight came. He opened his tent and very slowly stepped outside. As he approached the smoldering fire, he saw blood laying on the ground next to the chair Eric was sitting on. The handgun was laying on the ground covered with blood. Thomas looked around and could not see any trace of Eric.

Thomas packed his camp up and began his hike back to their car. As he walked slowly through the dense woods, he saw drops of blood along the trail. He walked what seemed to be miles until he saw something on the path way in front of him. As he approached it, he started screaming, it was Eric's arm mangled and covered with bugs.

Thomas started running as fast as he could down the trail. He heard something behind him. He looked back and saw a big animal running after him, catching up quickly. Thomas suddenly stopped. He realized he couldn't outrun the creature. He took aim as it darted toward him. Thomas fired his gun at the creature, hitting it as it fled into the woods, ending the chase. Thomas continued to run down the path toward the opening to the trail. He heard a loud scream, then saw another creature running quickly behind him.

Thomas thought I have to make it to the Jeep. As Thomas made it to the opening to the trail and ran to the Jeep. He dropped his keys. When he leaned to grab the keys, the creature also ran into the opening to the trail. Thomas gasped as he grabbed his keys and ran to the Jeep. He opened the door and jumped into the Jeep as the creature smashed out the side window. Thomas drove off as fast as he could, and the creature's arm wedged in the side door of the Jeep. The creature screamed and blood streamed onto the Jeep's floor. Thomas drove off with the creature's severed arm stuck in the door. Thomas was never seen nor heard from again.

The Vampire's Bronze Goblet

On April 14th 2014, a small group of explorers set out to explore a large cave system. They located the cave in the high mountains of Boulder, Colorado. The group was small. Gina, who knows a lot about nature, and Lawrence, who has explored and studied history, were there. Lawrence, led the hike to the top of the mountain. The day was cool and misty as the two made their way up the steep incline. Gina asked Lawrence once they reached halfway to the top of the mountain if they could stop and take a break.

As the two reached the midway point to the mountain top, they stoped to take a well-deserved break. Gina opened her backpack and started to eat some dried fruit and granola bars she had packed. Lawrence started to plan out the rest of the assent to the mountain top. Gina finished her break, then proceeded with Lawrence to the entrance to the cave.

As Gina and Lawrence entered the cave, the smell of rotting flesh overwhelmed them. Gina began to walk further into the cave as she suddenly tripped and fell. Lawrence yelled out Gina, are you OK? What happened? Gina replied, I tripped over something. As Lawrence shined a light on the object Gina tripped over, he gasped. Oh my God, Gina, what is this doing here. The object was a large bronze cross that had blood stains covering it.

A loud bang rang out. As Gina walked forward further into the cave, she saw a small part of the rock wall laying on the walk way. As she looked into an opening in the rock wall, she saw something shining. It was an old goblet resting into the rock wall as is someone carefully placed it there. Gina said, Hey Lawrence, this goblet has what looks to be blood in it. As Lawrence examined the goblet, he noticed a ring laying beneath the goblet. It appeared to be ancient and made of silver. Lawrence heard in the 1800s that vampires occupied the cave, so he informed Gina of his desire to visit. Lawrence told Gina that people from the town below went to the cave.

They killed and burned the vampires there, according to rumors.

He mentioned to Gina that people have rumored the cave to be very haunted from times past. Gina began to suddenly laugh at what Lawrence was telling her. Gina grabbed the goblet and yelled, hey Lawrence, If I drink this blood, will I turn into a vampire? As Gina quickly started to drink the blood from the goblet, Lawrence screamed No Gina, don't drink that!! Gina dropped the goblet and collapsed to the walk path. Lawrence grabbed Gina to help her.

Gina began to shake violently as Lawrence tried to help her. Gina started to stand up as Lawrence aided her. Oh my God, Gina, what's wrong with your hands. Ginas nails were extremely long and sharp pointed. As Gina looked into the face of Lawrence, he screamed and jumped back away from her. Gina, you are a vampire, Lawrence screamed as he ran down the walk path.

As Lawrence ran down the walk path, he began to notice skulls laying on the walk path. As he ran, he looked behind him as he saw a glimpse of Gina chasing him down the labyrinth of the cave. Lawrence saw the end to the cave closed, he screamed, Please Gina don't kill me I can help you. Lawrence stopped at the closed end of the cave as Gina slowly walked closer to him. Gina opened her mouth widely as Lawrence saw the pointed fangs as they leaned outward from her mouth. Gina, please no, screamed Lawrence. She spoke to Lawrence and told him if he brought people to the cave, she would spare his life. Lawrence said he would bring the people only if she would walk with him outside the cave.

Gina agreed to walk outside the cave with Lawrence as the sun had gone down. Lawrence walked outside the cave as Gina followed him. Lawrence walked to the steep edge of the mountain. He asked Gina to point out which part of the town below she wanted him to bring the people from. As Gina stood next to Lawrence and pointed at the small town. Gina suddenly let out a scream.

As she looked down at her chest, she saw Lawrence had driven a wooden stake deep into her heart. As Gina started to lose her balance, Lawrence said, I am sorry Gina, I can't let you harm the townspeople. Gina suddenly fell from the mountain's edge to the rocks below. As Lawrence slowly made his way down the mountain, the sun began to rise. As Lawrence descended the steep mountain side, he saw Gina's body turn to ash as the wind carried her ashes away. Lawrence only saw the remaining wooded stake aging on the ground.

The Winter Murderer

In the winter of 1995, a series of murders occurred in a small park in Vermont. The local police searched for the killer, but the leads ran cold. They found the bodies sitting on the park bench with their legs crossed. From a distance, it appeared that they were seated on the bench, relaxing.

The community was fearing the eerie murders that occurred in their town. One older gentleman named Jake lived in the town since he was young. Jake was known in the town as a mildly strange man. Jake, as a child, was seen screaming in the street as his Mother tried to get him to come into the house. The Mother of Jake was often seen leaving their home saying to Jake take deep breaths, Jake, everything is ok.

One Winter day, Jake was sitting on a bench in the park as one member of his community walked over and sat next to him. The woman who sat next to Jake tried to have a conversation with him. Jake just sat and did not reply, he only talked to himself in a soft voice. The woman said Jake it is cold out, I am getting numb on one side of my body. The woman said I don't feel well Jake, I have to go now.

Suddenly, Jake started laughing uncontrollably as the woman stood up. The woman let out a muffled sound as she tried to stand up, blood started pouring out of her side. As the woman fell to the ground motionless, Jakes hand shook as he held a knife in his hand. The glimmer from the blade was intoxicating to him as he watched the blood drip off the tip. Jake picked up the woman's body and placed her back on the bench and crossed her legs. Jack walked away from the scene quickly.

Jake didn't come back to the park for a while. Then he spotted an older man sitting alone on a bench, with the sun setting fast. Jake approached the man sitting and said, it is cold out today, isn't it, sir. The man replied yes, it is Jake. As Jake sat next to the man, he began to talk to the man about the community. He asked the man why the people of the town seemed to look at him like he was a circus freak or something.

The man told Jake he had to go, he forgot he had something to do. Jake said, come back tomorrow, I want to talk to you some more. He said he would come back tomorrow to keep speaking with Jake. Jakes facial expression changed as the man walked away toward his home. The next day, the man looked out his window. He saw Jake sitting on the park bench, staring at his house. The man walked slowly to the bench as Jake stared at him very intently. The man said, how are you today, Jake. Jake said nothing as he stared into the snow-white powder snow.

The man told Jake he would be right back, he had forgotten something in his house. The man watched Jakes expressions as he walked slowly to his house. It seemed like an eternity waiting for the man to come back to the park. Suddenly, the man exited his house and began walking toward Jake. As the man got closer to Jake, he asked Jake if he was cold. Jake responded to the man, he was not cold. The man and Jake had a long conversation as the day started to turn dark. As the man told Jake he had to leave, Jake screamed. The man said it's ok that Jake takes a deep breath as he walked away.

The next morning, the towns people saw someone laying on the ground near the bench in the park. The towns' people quickly called the police. As the police arrived, they ran over to investigate what had happened. As they turned the person over, blood spilled out of their coat. The townspeople started screaming. It's Jake, I can't believe it. A loud sound of laughter came from a distance away. It was the man standing in front of his house holding a bloody straight razor. I watched him kill us for years now, he will never kill us again.

The Crimson Red Ice Cream Cone

Several people reported that they went missing in the summer of July 1st, 1968. The police in Baltimore, Maryland are investigating some mysterious missing person cases. Reports came in of missing persons last seen talking to the area's soft serve ice cream man.

Henry was a 43-year-old man who grew up on the Chesapeake Bay all of his life. Henry took over the local ice cream man business after the passing of his Father. He stated many times he loved to walk along the bay and smell the brackish scent it produced. He also loved seeing local business signs downtown. Likewise, he loved the Dominos sugar sign. It had a bright orange glow that shined in the night sky. The community knew Henry as well as his family for many years.

One person came forward and recalled one day a little boy told his Father he wanted an ice cream from Henry. The Father scolded the little boy about eating too many sweets. As Henry looked at the Father, his entire face and body language changed. Henry began to grind his teeth and look extremely mad at the Father. The Father told his wife later that day what had happened and how Henry was staring at him. I think that is strange coming from Henry, don't you honey. The man stated for some reason he became afraid of Henry.

Two weeks later, the ice cream truck drove by the boy's Father's house and stopped. The man went outside to talk to Henry. The neighbor recalls seeing the boy's Father get into the ice cream truck with Henry and drive off. Days turned into weeks, the man was never seen again. The police received a call and drove to Henry's house to conduct their investigation.

As police started to Henry's front door, they heard screaming coming from his house. The police had their guns drawn and got to the front door. One police officer yelled Henry are you ok we are coming in. As the police entered Henry's house, they saw him sitting in a chair and laughing at a horror movie he was watching. Henry looked at the police and started to yell, why are you in my house, I did not invite you in, get out. As the police calmed Henry down, they started to ask him about the man who got into his ice cream truck.

Henry said he asked me for a ride out of town. I took him to a diner and dropped him off. The police asked Henry what street did you drop him off at. He replied, I don't know what street the diner is on. The police told Henry the man never returned home. Henry said all I know is I dropped him off at the diner and I drove back home. The police asked for permission to search his house. Henry stated that was fine. The police searched for what seemed to be an eternity. Ok Henry, we are going to go now, we might have questions for you later.

The next day, Henry started doing his ice cream route as he always did. As Henry saw the kids running to get to the ice cream truck, he began to laugh. The children ran to get to the side of the ice cream truck as Henry opened the small glass window. Henry told the children it was a special day. He said no one could stop them from having ice cream anymore.

He said he wanted to reward them with a custom flavor because they had always been good to him. The children yelled in cheer as Henry began to start the ice cream machine to make the ice cream for the children. As the first cone came out, Henry said you may need more napkins for my special flavor kids. One child held the cone. Another child screamed because their hand was bleeding. The parent grabbed the child, thinking somehow he cut his hand.

The parents wiped the blood from the ice cream cone and realized it came from the boy's hand, which was not cut. As the children looked at Henry, blood covered his hands as it dripped down the small window. Henry screamed I killed the boy's father that yelled at him for wanting an ice cream cone. Now he will never yell at him again. The people ran from the ice cream truck and called the police. Henry walked to the driver's side of the ice cream truck and laughed until the police arrived. As the police drove Henry away, the children with blood stains watched in horror.

The Dark Small Cabin

In 1997, Will, an outdoorsman, went into a big forest to find adventure during the summer. The weather was hot but somewhat dry. Will decided to take the trail that leads to a small cabin. The cabin is about 8 miles (ca. 13 km) away. Will be very fit and have no problem with a hike that far. While Will enjoyed the walk, he also knew about the danger of bears, cougars, and rattlesnakes. The person will carry a rifle and a 44 magnum handgun. As Will rounded a bend in the trail, he noticed a large Grizzly Bear walking down the trail toward him.

Will began to back up as he hid behind a large tree. He immediately reached for his 44 magnum as the bear approached. The Bear did not notice Will at first and slowly walked past the tree Will was hiding behind. Will watched the large bear walk past him and down the trail. As Will ran towards the small cabin, the bear followed him down the trail. He knew the small cabin was close if he could just get to it.

The cabin was in eyesight now as Will sprinted to it. As Will looked back, the large Grizzly was gaining on him from behind. Will could see the mouth open of the large Grizzly as it sprinted as well after Will. He was about 30 yards (ca. 27 m) from the cabin door. As he ran, he tripped and fell to the ground, the Grizzly was now upon him. Will grabbed his 44 as the Large Grizzly opened its mouth to attack Will. Someone heard a shot, and the bullet narrowly missed the giant head of the bear. The Grizzly quickly ran away from Will down the trail. He got up from the ground and ran to the cabin door.

As Will entered the small, dark cabin, the heavy, musty smell hit him. He walked to a minimal window to open its shutters to let in some light. The day turned into evening as Will started to unload his backpack full of food and supplies. As Will made his food, he wondered if the bear would return. As he rested into the light, he suddenly heard rustling from the rear of the cabin. He got up and grabbed his rifle and went slowly to the cabins' door. He looked out of the cracks between the wooden door and saw a large Cougar walking around the cabin.

The moonlight provided just enough light for Will to see. As he peered through the gaps in the cabin door, he saw a big eye staring back at him. Will moved away from the door as the cougar began to strike the door with its powerful paws. The door seemed to be taking a beating as the cougar clawed the door trying to gain access inside. Will aimed his rifle at the cabin door and shot through the door. The Cougar ran off quickly out of sight. Will did not sleep the rest of the night, not knowing if the Cougar would come back.

The next morning, Will rested and eventually began to get his belonging together. He thought he would walk to a small stream nearby. He would rather not venture too far away from the safety of the cabin. Will opened the cabin door as he looked around before exiting the entrance of the cabin. Gasping, Will see a dead deer lying on the ground close to the cabin, torn into pieces.

The cougar must have killed the deer. Will grabbed the deer by the legs because he did not want the cougar coming back around for the carcass. He dragged the deer far down the trail until he thought it was far enough from the cabin. Will began his journey to the small stream. It was only a small hike from the cabin, and Will wanted the fresh water that it would provide him with.

As Will walked to the stream, he felt nervous for some reason. He finally made it to the stream and began to fill his canteen with the fresh water. He saw small game across the stream he could use for food. Will got his rifle and carefully aimed at the small game.

As Will prepared to shoot the small game, he heard a noise and looked behind him. It was a Grizzly bear looking at him. Will pointed his rifle at the gigantic bear as he slowly backed up to cross the stream behind him to get away. The bear started to slowly move toward Will as he fired his rifle to scare the Grizzly. The bear swiftly ran into the forest and was not seen again.

Will decided it would be a wise decision to leave the stream area now he already had his water and did not feel safe. He walked away from the stream until he saw a small rock cave structure. As he began to climb the small cliff to the cave, he saw something in between one of the rocks. As the rattlesnake went to strike Will's hand that was close to where the rattlesnake was hiding. The snake just missed Will's hand. As the rattlesnake went to recoil, Will grabbed his knife and quickly severed the head of the snake. Will climbed to the top of the cliff to the entrance of the cave. Will see something move beneath the cliff. It was a cougar looking up at him as it began to climb the cliff towards Will.

He began to run inside the cave as he had drawn out his 44 magnum. Will ran for what felt like a very long time. Finally, he reached the end of the cave and noticed there was only one way out. He began to run back to gat out of the cave, he suddenly saw the cougar making its way to the entrance of the cave.

As Will stopped and locked eyes with the cougar. At that time, he knew this would not be his last stand. The cougar started to run towards Will as he aimed at the cougar. The 44 magnum Will had jammed. He reached for his knife. As the cougar lunged towards Will, he braced himself as he slashed the cougar's side. The cougar landed next to Will and was not moving. He ran down to the entrance of the cave and realized it was his faith and perseverance that saved him. Will continued the hike back and left the forest to never return again.

I wrote this story for my brother Will. He faced many challenges in his life. He has always succeeded due to his unparalleled perseverance.

The Underwater Sea Caves

A team of scuba divers went diving on July 7th, 1956. Locals believed that they explored cursed underwater caves. The location is Baja California. The group of divers stops for the night at a local motel near the dive site. The Motel staff asked the men what they were doing. The men state they are going to dive in the underwater caves the next day. The staff in the motel warn the men of the curse on the underwater caves. The men laugh and inquire about the location of the nearest restaurant. The motel staff said to go a little farther down the road and enjoy the food. They warned that if you go diving in the caves tomorrow, it might be your last meal.

The four men drive down the road and stop at a small diner to eat. The men get out of the vehicle. They see people inside the diner looking at them through the windows. One diver said, do you see that? People are staring at us through the windows. The other diver, John states, I see them, let's just eat our food then go.

When John and the other divers went into the diner, the waitress told them to sit elsewhere. One of the divers, Robert, asked do we have to sit here. The waitress said they should sit there. The locals knew they would explore the cursed caves tomorrow. The waitress informed them that the locals believed the men might be cursed. The men want to dive in the caves. She stated that news here travels very fast. Just ignore the people and eat some food.

The following day, the four men arrive at the location of the underwater caves. As the group started to unpack the dive gear for the dive. John sees someone walking down the beach toward them. The man stopped and asked the men if they were really going to dive the curse caves. Robert replied yes, we are diving the caves today.

The man stated to them, If they become afraid, search for the help of the mermen that may be around the caves entrance. John and Robert began to laugh at what the man just said. When he was young, the man was swimming near the cave entrance. Something grabbed him and tore off his arm. He blacked out, as he regained consciousness, he saw mermen dragging him back to the beach. As they placed him on the beach, they disappeared back into the sea.

As the man walked away from them, Robert and John just looked at each other and continued to unpack the scuba gear. John noticed something breaking the surface of the water at the entrance to the caves. He thought maybe his mind was playing tricks on him because of what the man said to them. The men had their scuba gear on and proceeded down the sandy beach to the water. One of the men stopped and told John he could not go with them to the caves. While John was asking if he was ok, another one of the divers said he also would not join on the cave dive.

John stated to them, what is the matter with you guys, we said we are going to dive here. David and Richard, two of the other divers, said to John they talked and decided not to dive at this location. David told John he did not feel good about the dive at the underwater caves. John said to David and Richard, that's fine. Robert, do you still want to do this with me? Robert stated he would go with John. As the two men entered the water, Richard and David stayed on the beach.

As John and Robert headed towards the cave, they saw something emerge from the water. The men swam to the opening to the cave and started their descent underwater into the cave. Robert looks at his gages, they read 25 meters down. The two see the opening to the cave. As they swim into the opening, they see something go past them quickly. John could not tell what it was that went past the men. Robert looked at his gages now they are at 50 meters deep.

The men start to explore the underwater cave. John follows Robert into a smaller opening into another section of the cave. As the two looks around inside the walls of the cave. They notice dive lines along the walls of the cave. Robert reaches out and grabs the lines to follow them to see where they go. As John and Robert follow the lines to see where they go, they see some large fish swimming around inside the cave. As the men watch the large fish swim around, suddenly the fish dart away, as if something in the cave spooked them. Robert and John keep following the dive lines until they reach a smaller opening in another cave. Inside the smaller opening hang large seaweed pieces from the interior walls of the cave.

As The divers enter the smaller opening to the cave, John sees something shining beneath him. As John uncovers the item, it appears to be an old wristwatch. Robert starts to look around with John to try to find other items on the cave floor. He sees something else shining on the bottom. It's a gold necklace laying on the bottom under some seaweed. The men continue to search for more jewelry laying on the bottom of the cave.

As Robert feels along the bottom, he hits something with his hand. He grabs the item and frees it from the silt built up on the bottom. It's a small metal jewelry box. As the box tilts, Robert sees the glimmer of its contents as it falls to the bottom of the cave. He starts picking up gold rings and places them into his wetsuit. The two men keep looking to find more jewelry. John looks along the cave wall and sees something.

John swims over to investigate what he sees. Robert stops behind John in disbelief. It's several skeletons along the cave walls. All the skeletons are wearing scuba gear. The two men noticed the diving gear that the deceased divers wore was ancient. Robert saw something sticking out of one of the diver's pockets. It was a large tooth of some kind. John saw big teeth in the wetsuit of the dead person's skeleton.

Robert saw some divers holding different items. One was holding a speargun and another was holding a divers knife. He thought about what was happening down here. He signaled to John to leave the cave. Something told Robert to take the speargun from the skeleton's hands. As John and Robert left the cave, they felt strange, like they were being watched.

The men found the divers' lines and started to follow them back out of the cave. As John looked back behind him through the small cave opening, he saw something move. John pushed Robert in front of him and signaled him to exit fast. As the two followed the lines as fast as they could, John again saw something move behind them. All of a sudden, a big snake-like creature swiftly came out from behind the men. The creature was moving fast toward the two men.

Robert put the spear gun out in front of him. The creature stopped and was moving slowly. The scales on the creature were nothing like the men had ever seen before. Jagged diamond shaped scales standing outward. They saw rows and rows of long teeth as the creature flowed water through its mouth out of gills on its side. The eyes are huge and a pointed like horn on its head. John saw a spear sticking out of one of its fins. The divers began moving along the diver lines, keeping their eyes on the slow sea creature.

The sea creature suddenly darted toward John with its mouth open. John pulled out his dive knife in an attempt to ward off the sea creature. The creature curved around John to get at Robert. He stabbed the creature in its head with the end of the speargun. As Robert struggled with the sea creature, John shot toward the entrance to the cave.

The creature violently shook back and forth to remove the spear from its head. Someone knocked Robert down. The creature fled back to the small cave opening. John swam back when he saw what happened to Robert. John went to Robert and helped him to the opening to the cave. As the two men left the cave and went into the water, Robert looked back. He saw a sea creature coming out of a cave underwater, swimming towards them. John went in front of Robert with his dive knife in his hand. The men suddenly saw something large moving up fast behind the sea creature.

The two men saw a sea creature coming toward them. The creature stopped and turned toward the cave. A large group of human – like mermen came up behind the sea creature. As the creature looked forward at the two men, it launched its attack on them again. The mermen quickly formed a wall between the creature and the men. The mermen began an attack of spears against the creature. John and Robert started toward the beach as the creature turned and sped to the cave, as the mermen followed. Richard and David dove into the water to help the two men. Until now, the cave's curse remains.

The Sirens Of The Bay

In New England lies a small town near the bayside. According to the local townspeople, Sirens plague the bay. The Aquatic creatures seem to come and go in the bay. During summer, the Sirens sometimes come up from the water and make fish go towards the shore. Recently, the Sirens have driven the fish further away from the bayside. The fishermen have tried nets to keep the Sirens from getting close to the shore line.

The creatures have shredded the nets into pieces. A terrible attack befell one fisherman. The fisherman was drawing in a net as a Siren launched an attack from the rear. The Siren's fins cut the man, and it severely bit him several times on the side and lower jaw area of his face. The men started to fish in larger groups to ward off any Sirens. In the Summer of 1994, the Sirens seemed to vanish without a trace. The fish soon returned to the bay in larger numbers than before. The fishermen had more than enough fish to sustain them.

The fish returning to the bay in huge numbers thrilled the fishermen. For countless years, the town thrived without spotting a single Siren in the bay. As months turned into years, the town's people wondered where the Sirens had gone. The fishermen often told tales of years gone by and how the Sirens caused an all out war with the local fishermen. The bay waters seemed calm and abundant with life. The men gathered to celebrate the plentiful bounty the bay had provided them.

The people in the town called a meeting to talk about what to do if the Sirens came back. John was the eldest member of the town and the community looked to him for advice. As John spoke, the townspeople listened, the room was dead silent as he spoke. John stated the fishermen would try to live in peace with the Sirens if that was possible. He stated, even if the attempts in the past years were unsuccessful, they needed to try again for the town. One man stood up and shouted, those water devils took my son and shedded him to death. I can't and will not ever forget what they did to my boy.

The man promised to seek revenge on every Siren he saw in the bay. He would never show mercy to the water creatures. John told the man he could never understand what he was going through with the loss of his son. He stated to the man he should honor his son by trying to make peace with the Sirens for the town's sake. The men of the town decided when the Sirens would return, John would attempt to make peace with the Sirens.

One early morning on July 12th 1996, the fishermen set out as any other normal fishing day. The Bay water was eerily very calm. The shine on the water was almost blinding, as not a ripple on the water's surface was visible. The men started preparing the fishing gear and cutting the bait for the day's fishing. One young man was standing toward the stern side of the vessel as the other men prepared to start fishing. As the young man leaned over as if to gaze into the water.

The men asked him what he was doing, they needed help with the gear. He said, "I'm just looking at the water." He stared into the deep water and saw a creature's face come up. Likewise, he started to scream, the Sirens, he yelled. The other fishermen ran to his side as the face of the creature had disappeared into the depths. The men asked the young man what was he talking about, they saw nothing. The men asked the man to go below deck and rest, perhaps because he was tired.

The men began casting the lines out for the day's catch of fish. The men shortly starting catching fish one line at a time. The fish seemed larger than the fish they had caught before. One of the fishermen said, wait a minute, this is a different species of fish that is only found in very deep water. The man said these fish are not from our bay. He stated to the men what made the fish enter the shallower waters of the bay. One man yelled, who cares fish is fish, let's take all we can. As the men continued to pull as much fish as possible out of the bay. Someone spotted a large ripple on the water's surf and saw a Siren breaching the surface.

Suddenly, large waves started to form around the fisherman's vessel. Sirens began to surface around the vessel. At first, the creatures were moving slowly through the water. Suddenly, the water creatures began darting quickly around the vessel as it began to rock. The men started to grab harpoons as they panicked. John, the eldest town member, screamed, no men, this is not what we want. We need to try to make peace with the Sirens. John stoped the men from engaging the creature with the harpoons. He said he would try to go to the bow of the vessel to somehow try to contact the creatures.

The men warned him that he should not trust the creatures and that this was a terrible idea. John walked to the front of the boat and saw a big Siren emerging from the water. The larger Siren made a loud sound, and the other Sirens disappeared beneath the waves. John began to reach out a hand as if to touch the creature. As the creature began to descend the waters, John's hand touched the surface of the water. John turned to the men and said, you see they are not at all dangerous. John screamed as a gigantic wave appeared. A Siren jumped out of the water and cut off his arm.

The fishermen quickly took John below deck for medical help, while the others yelled to get armed. One man yelled, kill as many of the creatures as you can, men. The men began to throw harpoons, hitting the larger Siren that had injured John. The Large Siren made a horrible sound as blood began to pour out of the creature's side. The men yelled, we killed it, let's head back to shore right away. The boat turned and headed back to shore. A gigantic line of ripples appeared behind the vessel as it moved towards the shoreline.

Sirens seemed to come from everywhere as they sped toward the boat. It seemed to be hundreds of the creatures. The men screamed, get us to shore quickly. The Sirens circled the vessel as they started their attack on the vessel. The men stared to throw harpoons at the creatures. The creatures began slashing the vessel with their tails. The vessel suffered severe damage. The men started stabbing the creatures with the ends of the harpoons as the bay began to turn dark red.

The men fought the Sirens while noticing a large wave forming farther behind the boat. A big Siren came up and made a loud sound. The other creature quickly went underwater. The big Siren swiftly swam to the back of the ship. The men threw harpoons to stop its attack. The creature shot to the surface of the water as it smashed the vessel into two pieces.

The men screamed as they were thrown into the bay. The sirens started once again to come from all directions as the men were being attacked. The creatures shredded the limbs of the men in the water. The sound the men made as they were being killed by these creatures was deafening. John saw one of the men grasping a large piece of what was left of his vessel.

The men grabbed John and began to swim toward shore. The shore did not seem that far away as the men swam to reach the shoreline. The shoreline was about 60 yards (ca. 55 m) away as the men saw the sirens start to race toward them. The two men in the water were quickly surrounded by the Sirens, who the men thought would kill them. The Large Siren approached the men as John began to look into the creature's eyes. John stared at the creature's eyes for what seemed to be an eternity. The creature made a loud sound as John and the other man thought they were going to loss their lives.

The Sirens disappeared beneath the waves. As John was still staring at the large Siren, it slowly went beneath the waves as it looked back towards him. The two men made it to shore as the townspeople grabbed the men out of the water. Until now, John tells the townspeople, do not overfish our bay and leave the Sirens alone. John thought the fishermen overfished the bay. As a result, the deep water fish came out. The Sirens chased them into the bay. We have taken too much from the bay and must only take what we need and nothing more. We can live together in peace with the Sirens as long as we don't overfish.

The Haunting Of Apartment 8907

On June 18th 1990, a young engaged couple searched for an apartment in Baltimore. The couple found an apartment and put in an application. The next week, someone from the apartments called to congratulate the couple on their new home. Ken and Marie began moving into their new apartment and strange things began to happen. Ken noticed a cold spot in the hallway toward the one back bedroom. Marie started to unpack some of her belongings. The couple noticed objects in the apartment start to move around. Ken and Marie unpacked until they got tired. They decided to finish unpacking the next day.

The next day, Ken made breakfast for Marie. Then, he started unpacking their things to find the TV. After they unpacked, they would take a walk around the apartment complex. Later that night, the couple went to sleep, and we're awakened by a man's voice letting out a scream. The sound was as if someone had been in pain. Marie jumped up and stared at the bedroom. I saw a small blue, white light pattern moving across the wall. The temperature in the back bedroom would change as the blue white light disappeared. The next day, Marie told Ken she would rather not elaborate on the events that happened. Marie thought that the events would get worse if they talked about them.

The next night, Marie said goodbye to Ken because she had to go to work. Ken thought a nice hot bath would be relaxing. As he entered the back bedroom to the bathroom, he felt a cold spot in the bedroom. Ken got undressed and ran the water. He sat in the bathtub and started to try to relax. Suddenly, the sound of people talking in the front room surprised him. Ken grabbed a towel and went to the front room to find the television on, playing loud.

Ken turned the television off and sat in the chair. He saw a blue, white light orb in the reflection of the television screen in front of him. As the time passed, he started to feel sleepy. Ken entered the back bedroom and put his pajamas on. He then laid in the bed and started to doze off. Suddenly, Ken saw the blue, white orb appearing in the corner of the room. The room's temperature suddenly became cold. An unknown force suddenly pushed the end of the mattress, causing Ken to feel it. As Ken started to become afraid, the mattress pushed in next to him. Just as if someone laid in the bed next to him. The dog started to growl and look toward the bathroom door. Ken jumped up out of the bed and before he could turn on the light. The blue white orb light shot quickly across the room. The room started to become warm again.

The next day, Ken did not say a word about the terrifying events that occurred. Ken made breakfast as usual and started to watch television. Ken received a candle from his mother on his birthday. He went into the living room area to light it. Ken could not light the candle, the automatic lighter had fluid in it, was new. He smelled a strange smell. As he entered the kitchen, he saw all the gas burners turned on with no pilot light. Ken shut off all the burners and ran out the sliding glass door to the outside. How did this happen, Ken thought the burner knobs had locks on them?

The couple noticed someone moving things in the apartment. We had placed pillows in different areas of the apartment. As the couple lived in the apartment for a year and a half, they wondered what happened here? Ken saw a neighbor leaving his apartment. The man lived directly across from Ken and Marie's apartment.

Ken told the man about the events that happened. The man said he had similar things happening. He told Ken he did not know what it was, but assured Ken it would not harm them. Ken went to the rental office to pay the rent. He asked the lady there if anything happened at the apartment. The woman told him she lived in the area since she was a young girl. The woman recalled the land that the apartment complex sits on used to be an old clay mine many years ago.

Ken returned to the apartment. He thought, could this be why the strange events happening? Ken heard the sound of water running. He ran to the back room to find water coming from the bathroom. The bathtub was overflowing. He turned off the faucet and grabbed towels to get the water up. What the hell is happening, he thought? Ken started to look up ways to try to rid the apartment of the spirit or spirits that dwelled here. He would not tell Marie about trying to rid of the spirit. Ken walked around the apartment when Marie was at work, speaking out bible verses.

He went to sleep that night, nothing happened. Ken thought what he did must have worked. Marie came home and they enjoyed a day out. As night fell, Marie kissed Ken goodbye to leave for work. As Marie left for work, Ken listened to music on the radio. He went to make something to eat. The lights in the kitchen started to come on and off. Suddenly, the volume on the stereo went loud. Ken turned off the radio and spoke in a loud voice, you are not welcome here. I command you to go away. The room fell quiet and Ken did not feel a negative presence.

Ken went to bed around 1:15 am and heard a loud bang on the bedroom wall. He jumps up, scared, and stood looking toward the bathroom. Ken heard the bang again coming from the bathroom. He slowly entered the bathroom, seeing the blue, white orb shoot past him as he entered. The bathroom temperature changed quickly. The following day, Ken told Marie what was happening while she was at work. The couple decided it would be best to leave the apartment. The next week, the couple left the apartment, never to return. Apartment 8907 is the setting for the true events that occurred. We change the names to protect the people's identity.

The Haunted Victorian Manor

On June 8th, 1976, a large victorian manor went up for sale by the owner. Within four days, the first set of potential buyers came along. Frank and his wife Liz and son John had been searching for a new home for some time. The couple stumbled upon it by seeing a sign for it as they passed through the area to visit friends. Frank contacted the owner of the property to set up a time to see the home.

The owner, Ray, told Frank anytime is fine, just please call ahead. Frank called Ray on a Thursday morning to set up a time to see the manor. Ray replied now is ok if you have the time today. Frank said he would come to the manor at about 12:00 pm. Ray said that would be fine. As Frank and his family pulled up to the Manor, his wife Liz was smiling. The three got out of the car and walked up the large wooden staircase to the front doors.

The owner Ray opened the large arched wooden doors and let the family enter the large manor. As Frank was talking to the owner, Liz started to look around the large manor. She walked up the big wooden stairs, made by skilled woodworkers. The remarkable beauty of the manor took Liz. From the incredible hand carved wood staircase to the marble flooring. As the family looked around the manor, John was standing in the parlor staring at the corner. Liz saw John and walked out of the room with him. Suddenly, they heard another vehicle driving up to the manor.

Frank asked the owner if other people were coming to see the manor today as well? Liz said to Frank she wanted the manor before someone else bought it. The owner told them he had to tell them something before they decided to buy the manor. The owner stated that they reduced the price of the home due to the tragedy that happened there. Someone with an axe killed a family of five. They found their bodies hidden in the cellar. Liz said she did not care, she still wanted the house.

John was walking and speaking with someone as he walked through the manor. Liz said John, who are you talking to? Alfred is John's reply. He used to live here a long time ago, mommy. Liz told John he would have to go now they had to find daddy.

As Liz and John found Frank, he was signing papers with the owner. The house is yours now, Frank. The Owner said to Liz as he passed to leave his home for the last time. The manor picked you, Liz, and he laughed. As the day quickly turned into night, Frank said the family should celebrate the new home. Frank had bought the home fully furnished. He told Liz they can buy other furniture if she wanted because what was there was old. "Liz replied" no, I want it to stay original as possible, Frank.

Frank felt tired. He went up the big wooden stairs to rest in the upstairs rooms. Liz ran upstairs to tell Frank she just saw a man walking down the stairs to the cellar. Frank descended quickly down the staircase to see who went into the cellar. He slowly went into the cellar and looked around. No one was there, Liz, maybe you need some rest, it has been a long day.

The family finally went to bed after a long day. The sound of someone crying downstairs suddenly awakened Frank. It sounded as if it were a female's voice. Frank got a flashlight and started slowly going down the stairs. Frank saw a strange woman standing in the parlor. The woman had blood covering her and was crying. The woman looked at Frank and slowly walked to the cellar door. As she turned back to look at Frank, she vanished. Frank went down in the cellar to look around. Frank did not see anything. He could only smell a slight hint of lavender. Frank returned to bed thinking about what he had just seen downstairs.

The family settled into the manor, and Frank went to the cellar. He wanted to know why the mysterious couple went there. As Frank walked across the stone floor, he stepped on a loose stone. He bent down and removed the stone. Something was under the stone wrapped in a bloodstained cloth. Frank uncovered what looked to be a small tin box with a small lock on it. He saw something shining in the dirt in the hole. It was a small key to the tin box. He took the tin box upstairs to show Liz.

Liz looked at the box and told Frank, maybe he should just put the box back under the stone and leave it alone. He sat the old tin box on a table in the parlor while he thought of what to do with it. As Frank returned to the old tin box. The tin box was gone. Frank asked John and Liz if they had seen the box, they said no. As Frank returned to the cellar, he noticed someone had placed the stone back over the hole. As if he had never removed it at all, he unwrapped the bloodstained cloth to reveal the stone and the old tin box.

Frank determined to discover the contents of the tin box. He went into the cellar and removed the stone. Frank took the small metal key and opened the tin box. The box was full of jewelry, a man's ring and several women's necklaces. Frank tried on the ring and it fit his finger. The ring was silver and had a large blood-red stone set into the top. Frank left the tin box opened on the stone floor of the cellar and returned to the upper levels of the manor.

Frank started to feel a little strange. He thought perhaps he had too much excitement for one day and went to lay down for a while. As Frank lay in the bed, he heard a woman's voice say you found the ring, my darling. Frank got out of bed and returned downstairs to tell Liz what had happened.

John woke up in the middle of the night. As he got out of bed, he noticed a line in the wall covering on the wall. He placed a small table where he walked over. John moved the small table to reveal a hidden door. As the small boy opened the door and entered. Suddenly, John heard the voice of the little boy Albert that used to live in the manor. "Hey John" come and play with me. John walked toward the voice and saw Albert standing with a woman covered with blood. John, terrified, started running away. "John it's ok replied Albert" this is my mommy, her name is Elizabeth. She won't hurt you, it's ok.

John walked back to Albert and started to play with him. Albert told John they should play hide and seek in the large manor. Albert went first to hide from John in the house. John started down a long hallway to find Albert. As he walked to find Alberts hiding place, he came upon another door. John started to open the door and heard a loud moan come from inside the room. He slammed the door and ran down the hallway.

Suddenly, he found Albert holding hands with the blood covered woman. "John yelled" something grabbed his shoulder. It was Frank, his father, what are you doing? Look dad, this is my friend Albert and his mommy Elizabeth. As John turned back, no one was there. Frank led his son John out of the room and blocked the door with a larger piece of furniture. Do not venture into areas of this house without me, John. When Frank went back to the parlor, he saw the woman covered in blood. She walked through the parlor and headed towards the cellar.

Frank went to the cellar to get the tin box and clean up the cellar a little. As Frank went to one corner of the cellar, he slipped and fell against the stone wall. A stone fell out of the wall, Frank got up off the floor and noticed the stone that had fallen out of the wall.

He began to place the stone back into the wall when he noticed something in the wall. Frank ran upstairs and got his flashlight. As he shined the light into the open hole caused by the stone falling out of the wall. Frank saw an old axe tucked into the wall.

He ran upstairs and called the local police. The family waited for the local police to arrive. The police went into the old cellar and retrieved the old axe. The officer told Frank they would have to keep the axe to run testing on it. The following week, the police called Frank and confirmed that the axe was the murder weapon. Someone used it to kill five family members. Frank began to get chills.

After the family had dinner, they decided that moving out of the manor was the best choice. All three family members went to bed as usual. The following morning, Frank and Liz packed as John was still asleep upstairs. Frank finished packing the family's belongings by 12:00pm. He climbed the big staircase and saw his son John holding hands with Albert. Blood covered his mother. "Frank gasped" John, I need you to come with me.

John told Albert he had to go with his father. As Frank quickly walked with John, he looked back as they disappeared. The Family got into the car and started to drive away. Frank asked John what happened. "John replied" they said they can rest now because you found the axe in the wall. John saw Albert in the window of the manor and waived goodbye to him. The family never returned to the victorian manor again.

The Eerie Playground

On a gloomy, fog covered evening, a middle-aged man went for a walk. The man thought going for a bit of fresh air would be good for him. The fog was thick, which is not uncommon for an evening in London. The man walked for what seemed to be an eternity. As he rounded a bend, he began to feel uneasy for some reason. Suddenly, the sound of children laughing filled the air. David, the middle-aged man, had no

Idea where the sound was coming from. As David walked, he noticed a child's shoe laying on the side of the walk path.

He continued walking, the walk path can to a fork. David thought should I take the right path or the left path. David took the right path, as David walked, the path opened to a small roadway. He stopped to look both ways before crossing the roadway. He saw across the road was the other side of the walking path. As David began to walk across the road path, suddenly a small car came speeding down the road way. David looked at the fast car and the headlights blinded him for a moment. David screamed, the car sped past.

He was thrown to the road way. He noticed his torn clothes as he got up from the road way. David was fine, but his clothes did not fair as well. He continued on his walk and felt pain in his right arm. He looked down and saw he had a small laceration on the inner side of his right arm. David thought it was just a scratch, considering what had just happened. The walk began to feel somehow different. The long walk would eventually lead David to an old playground.

As David gazed at the large old playground, he began to hear the laughter of children. He noticed a bench outside the playground. David sat on the bench and looked at the interior of the eerie playground. David saw children playing a game called ghost in the graveyard ein the playground. He started to feel cold as he watched the children play. The children appeared to be relatively transparent.

David saw the swings on the playground moving with no one on them. The laughter of the children strangely became loader and louder as the time pasted. David suddenly became tired, as if something dark covered him and had taken all the energy from his body. The time seemed to go by very slowly as David watched the children play. One child was staring at David and laughing as he pointed at him.

David sat on the bench, confused, as a small child laughed and pointed at him. The other children played nearby. The child suddenly stopped laughing and pointing and began to walk toward David. The child called out to David, you can see us playing, sir.

Yes, David told the small child, I can see you very well. The small child told David his name was Peter and he been in the playground for a very long time. The small boy walked away and started to chase around the other children. David sat for a while longer as he watched the children play. As David began getting exhausted, almost sleepy, he decided to begin to take his long walk back to his flat.

David started walking as he strangely felt a very eerie feeling come over him. David kept walking until he reached the road. He noticed it was completely quiet. He walked what seemed to be miles and miles. David walked down the pathway. He thought he was tired because his vision was slightly blurry.

Was it the right path or the left path. David took the right path and walked until he came upon the small child's shoe. He gasped as he gazed upon the small child's shoe covered with blood dripping down the laces. David began to run down the walk path frantically.

David ran down the path to his flat. He heard children laughing, growing louder and louder. David thought what was going on with me. When I return to my flat, I must acknowledge that I am tired and in need of some rest. He ran down the pathway and suddenly saw children running around him as he traveled down the pathway.

All the children were laughing and pointing at David as he ran. As David oddly stopped and looked at his watch, the time was half past midnight. How can it be so late, David thought? As David looked up, he saw the children standing near him, just staring. David screamed, go and play and leave me alone now.

As one of the children walked toward David, he said, "Sir, we can't leave you here. We sent ourselves to bring you with us." He felt pain suddenly in his side. David screamed when he opened his jacket and saw his bloody ribs sticking out. The children started to laugh, you don't know sir, you did not survive the car that struck you on the roadway.

A Haunting In Rome

The year is May 1st 2016 I am traveling to Rome for the first time. My name is Anthony, I have received this gift from my parents for my 19th birthday. I have always had a fascination with Roman and Greek history. The day of my flight, my nervous level was high, perhaps I was overly excited about my trip. My parents escorted me to the airport to see me off. As I got on the plane, my parents waved goodbye. When I looked back, my mother's smile had disappeared, and she had a serious look on her face.

I sat by the window and took a deep breath. The airline attendant told us to fasten our seat belts before takeoff. The plane's engine's whirling sound was almost hypnotic. I closed my eyes as the plane thrusted forward to gain speed for the takeoff. As the plane ascended into the heavens, I felt an unusual calm. The journey to Rome seemed longer than I had expected.

As I stared out of the aircraft window, I could see a distant landing strip as we slowly descended out of the clouds. You could hear the aircraft flaps making a sound as it started to land. The airflow across the wings was changing slowly. The wheels screeched on the runway, making my hands grip the hand rest tighter. When the plane landed and started moving, I let out a loud sigh. I wasn't concerned about the others. I was happy to have landed safely.

As the plane came to a stop and the airline attendant's assisted passenger's off the plane. I was nervous as other people left the aircraft before I did. I thought, calm down Anthony, we have landed and just be patient. As my turn to depart the aircraft approached, I felt a calmness come over me as I stepped on Romes soil.

The smell of the air seemed different and somewhat dry. I walked to the nearest tour guide, as he had taken me to a place to stay for several days. The owners of the small house seemed friendly as they had me enter their home to stay a few days. I reached into my bag to pay for my stay, as the woman told me I could pay before my departure. The couple knew a bit of English and understood most of what we said. The couple asked if I was going to see the coliseum.

I replied yes, I would go in the afternoon to see the coliseum. The couple glanced at each other. Then the man leaned towards me and warned, "Beware the restless spirits of the men who died in the coliseum." As the night came and went, the couple was up early preparing my breakfast for me. The breakfast consisted of fresh buttered rolls and some red wine and olives. I thanked the couple as my tour guide was soon to arrive. As I walked out of the small house, a small car approached and the tour guide exited the vehicle.

The driver assisted me into the car as we drove to the coliseum. The traffic patterns of the road seemed strange as cars passed us. The image of the coliseum will be forever engraved in my memory as we pulled into an area to park. The size of this magnificent structure amazed me. It was built manually hundreds of years ago. The first tour guide gave me to the coliseums tour guide. I felt a cool breeze when I entered the big structure. As we walked into the middle of the coliseum, I was startled by the loud screams and cheers. I looked around, I saw a large gladiator running toward me with a sword and a shield.

I turned quickly to find the other tourists. No one was there. Only strange faces in the coliseum seats, yelling and screaming, "Kill him." As I turned, the gladiator was directly in front of me as he swung his large sword. I looked at my hand holding a sword. I raised my sword as the gladiators sword and mine clashed. The sound of the iron hitting one another was deafening. As I swung my sword, the gladiator's sword narrowly missed my head. In response, I swiftly struck back. The gladiator fell to his knees, blood gushing from his stomach. The wound was critical. As I dropped my sword, I thought I must be dreaming as the audience screamed kill him. As I stood and looked up, a man emerged from the upper level of the coliseum. Oh my God, it was Cesar pointing at me showing me a thumbs down, which means to kill the opponent.

I refused to raise my sword as Cesar looked away, he waved at the guards. As their swords were drawn, the guards of Cesar quickly surrounded me. As the guards grabbed me and forced to my knees. I saw the sunlight glimmer off the guard sword blade as he raised it to behead me. As he took his swing I closed my eyes the cheers fell silent, was I dead. As I opened my eyes, I was standing outside the coliseum as the tour guide asked me if I was ok. I went back to their house to get my things. They asked if I saw the gladiators and Caesar. I did see them, it seemed so real, not dreamlike at all. Furthermore, I went to pay the couple for the stay, but they did not accept the money. The woman stated you have seen quite enough. Keep your money and return to your country and stay safe. As I boarded the plane, the events will haunt me for eternity.

Devils Run Mountain

Living on devil's run mountain may seem scary to most people due to its history of ghosts. I have lived on devil's run mountain since I was a young boy. I have witnessed many unexplainable things. My name is Richard and I will share my story with you. One evening, as the cold winter air swept across the mountain side, I went to get wood for my fireplace. I chose a steep and dark path.

As I walked down the mountain, I heard something behind me, like someone following. Suddenly, I heard a loud crack behind me, and as I turned, I saw a man standing and looking at me. I gasped as I then realized it was a ghost. The clothing on the man was old and from another time. I turned quickly and started to run back to my cabin. When I reached the mountain peak, I noticed numerous ghosts near the cabin. It seemed like they were curious about the previous residents.

One of the ghosts turned around and looked toward my direction as I quickly hid behind some pine trees. As I stood in the chilled night air waiting for my chance to run to the cabin. The ghost of the man was rounding the turn on the path beneath me. I then though if I did not run toward the cabin, the ghost man will certainly see me hiding. As the ghost slowly began to get closer to my location. I ran from behind my hiding spot and ran toward the cabin. As I got closer to the door to the cabin, I fell to the cold ground as the spirits surrounded me. As the sun started to rise the next morning, I awakened in my bed. Was this a bad dream, as I entered the downstairs, the front door of the cabin was standing wide open.

I quickly shut and locked the cabin door. As the freezing cold air trickled through the small cracks of the cabin, I began to gather wood for the fire. As the fire was being started, I saw a figure behind me. I turned and screamed, it was the ghost man standing as he began to speak to me. Do not fear me, I saved your life from the others. I picked you up and quickly brought you inside as they began to surround you. I cannot stay with you and do not leave the cabin as I am certain they are waiting for you once again. The ghostly figure vanished. Daylight faded into evening. Richard pondered how to handle the spirits.

As he started to dose off to sleep, he sat near the warm fire, suddenly he heard a knock at the door of the cabin. He yelled who is it and what do you want from me. A soft voice said they wanted him to come outside the cabin. Richard yelled, you are not welcome here, please go away. As Richard yelled, he began to see the ghost coming to the windows of the cabin as if to look in upon him. He suddenly saw the ghost man appear. The ghost man started to yell no, we must leave this man in peace and never bother him again.

The night seemed an eternity as Richard slept off and on for hours. The next morning, the clock on the wall read 7:15am. Richard woke up to the sunlight coming through the slightly open curtain. He walked to the cabin door to look outside. As he opened the cabin door, a small cluster of wildflowers laid at its entrance. A small, slightly folded piece of paper lay next to it. As Richard picked the piece of paper up and began to read is, he gasped.

The paper read, I live on this mountain and have seen you many times. The cabin you're in has been empty for a while because it's haunted by eternal spirits. It seems the spirits have not returned since last night. The spirits of the dead have also come to my cabin every night for years. I know your family very well and actually had one of the spirits speak to me last night. The man spirit stated to me if you stay and take care of the cabin, the spirits will never return again.

Dining With A Queen Vampire

As the sun set in Manhattan, New York, people walked on the city's sidewalks. Their faces glowed in the last sunlight. As night fell, a beautiful woman appeared as she walked down the streets of Manhattan. Her gate as she walked was strangely calculated, almost seductive, as if she had no care in the world. As the people rushed around her, she had a smile with a slight grin. She paused in front of a fancy store and looked at the clothes in the window. Somebody at a café noticed her. The man had a look as if he were under a strange spell. The woman turned and looked at the young man with a smile as she motioned for him to come over to her. The man was in shock that a woman as beautiful as her would ever want him.

As the man walked across the street, gazing at the stunning woman in front of him, not looking at the traffic. A car stuck him and launched him into the air. As the tires of the car skidded, the driver tried to stop the car. The young man was laying motionless as the beautiful woman

          D.S. BANKERT

ran to his aid. The woman picked up the man as the shopkeepers had called the police. The man was coming in and out of consciousness. As his eyes opened slightly, he saw the beautiful woman's face start to become partially gray. He stated to the woman what happened to me.

The woman said, "A car struck you, and you need help." Please, the man stated, take me to a hospital. I am here to help you live forever, my dearest. As the man started to ask what she was talking about, he felt a sharp pain on the side of his neck. He felt a sharp pain in his neck, as if something was applying pressure. The pain seemed to tear the skin and enter a vein. As he started to pass out again, he saw the woman raise her head as blood fell from her mouth. She stated now you will never die and live as I do. You shall never age and will see the world with new eyes. As the woman spoke, she noticed the presence of the police getting closer to her. The woman stated to the man, we must leave this place now, my love.

As the woman picked the man up with bloodstained hands, she jumped with him to a buildings' rooftop. As the police searched for the young man, the beautiful woman waited for nightfall to leave the area. The man remained in the shadows until he opened his eyes again. As their eyes met, he screamed, noticing that her eyes appeared bright red, as if blood had coated her face. She covered his mouth as she said, I know, my love. I was terrified when my master remade me. I quickly realized who I was and what I needed to survive this new life.

The man started to sit up as the woman told him to rise slowly to adjust to his new life. As he stood, he soon became weak as he fell to the floor. The woman started to laugh uncontrollably. I am sorry my love, I remember the same thing happened to me the first time I stood after being a newly made vampire. The man screamed a vampire, what the hell did you do to me. The woman's hands had become lengthened and nails slightly pointed. I think you do not know what you have become.

One day, you will be glad I am your maker and your master. I am not just your master, I am the master of thousands of vampires who have started the same way you are. You should give me gratitude, not insults. The man screamed, what are you talking about, you are an undead monster. I am the Queen of the vampires, and tonight you will dine with me. I would rather die than dine with you, a useless creature of the night. Fine, stated the woman, the pain of increased hunger will become unbearable until you beg to dine with me. I will leave you for now, when you are ready to dine with me, just call out for me.

As time seemed to pass very slowly, the pain of hunger started to almost become crippling for the young man. He tried to fight the pain by attributing it to the queen vampire. Maybe she put it there subconsciously. The pain became overwhelming. He clawed the floor, blood seeping from his hands. He could not stand any more pain as he screamed out, queen help me now, please. The queen came into the room, laughing. She said, "I guess you're ready to eat with me now. You called me a useless creature of the night." As you rise, we will go and dine this night.

When he stood up, his eyes changed and his hands grew longer with pointed fingernails. The woman stated his eyes would now be able to see in complete darkness. As the two made their way into the night, the lights of the city became almost blinding to the man. The woman told him to wait with her in the shadow's until someone came close to them. She stated to him the first time for him would be difficult, but it was necessary to sustain his life. As a woman walked down the darkened ally, the woman told the man to stay silent until he strikes. As the woman walked down toward the two, the man started to hesitate. The woman's face turned dark gray as she pushed the man back and launched her attack. The woman turned to face the attacker.

The queen vampire deeply slashed her throat as she fell to the ground, bleeding out. The queen started to yell out hurry and drink before her heart stopped, you can never drink from the dead. As she was yelling at him to dine with her, he saw a part of an old wooden box next to him. He yelled, "I won't eat with you!" Then he broke the box and picked up a pointed piece of wood. He started to stab himself. The woman yelled, don't you want eternal life. The man yelled, not as a monster like you, as he plunged the wood into his heart. The woman lunged at him as he quickly turned to ash.

The Drain System

In the early fall of 2022 I went to work at 7:45am as I usually do. My name is David. I am Twenty years old. As I went to pull into a parking space at the grocery store I work at, I noticed a grate covering a large drainage system. I did not pay the drain any attention, but perhaps I should have. As I parked my car, a strange feeling washed over me, like something exciting was about to occur. As I began to exit my car, the unthinkable happened. It was as if it happened in slow motion. The glimmer of the sunlight off my keys as they fell to the drainage grates surface. I gasped as the keys balanced on edge as I lunged to save them from falling in the drain. The split second before my hand grabbed the keys, they fell to the bottom of the drain system. As the keys hit the water below, I yelled because I could not see them.

I frantically got a steel bar from my car to attempt to lift the heavy grate. The weight of the grate was intense as I struggled to lift it to enter the drain system. As I peered down into the partially dark drain system, I lifted the heavy grate. I took a deep breath as I slowly climbed down into the open chamber. The smell of the drain made me ill as I dunked my hands into the stagnated water, searching for my keys.

As I searched for the keys, suddenly my hand seemed to get sucked into a small opening in the drain. I screamed out in pain as I felt as if something bite into my hand. I stared in disbelief as the dark water turned red, and struggled to free my trapped hand from the hole. As the water's red color was almost gone, the pressure released my hand. I didn't realize right away that something had bitten off some of my fingers. I pulled my hand out. Furthermore, I screamed as the deafening sound of the heavy grate cover began to shift and close off my escape.

Besides, I tried to swim up with my injured hand, but the grate closed, narrowly missing my other hand.

Likewise, I yelled for help, but as I sat and waited for help, water started to pour into the area I was in. Likewise, I had to go down one of the drains to find a way out. Furthermore, I started to go down the right side drain as I heard something behind me. As I looked, a man with a deformed face surfaced as he was grabbing towards my legs as I kicked him. Furthermore, I yelled as I could not stand, only craw quickly away.

Besides, I made it to another opening as I saw the drain I was in open into four drains. The water behind me was moving, so I knew the deformed man was not far behind. As I rounded a corner, I spotted the deformed man round the corner as well. I quickly saw a small opening to hide in. As I squeezed into the narrow passage, the deformed man's face turned quickly around the corner.

It was if he was suddenly confused where I might have gone. Thankfully, he did not spot my hiding spot. As the man passed me into another drain. I started to exit my hiding spot as I heard the sound of as someone else was coming down the drain pipe we had just come from. I though, could, it is someone to help me? As I looked, a woman with decaying skin was crawling quickly behind the man with the deformed face.

I began to shake from fear that if they discovered my hiding spot, they would kill me. As the decayed woman passed me, I quickly came out from hiding and went back down the drain I knew I just came from. As I entered the drain that had the grate covering it, I saw a small car pull up next to it and began to park. A man was exiting the vehicle.

I began to scream out, help me, I am stuck in this drain. The man's head turned quickly towards me, and he ran to the grate cover. There is something down here, and I hurt, please help me get out. The man said he would be right back, he had to get something to open the grate. As

I saw the man returning, I saw the water movement behind me, It was the decaying woman as she crawled towards me.

The woman's jaw was partially hanging down as her gaped mouth was open. I screamed for the man to get me out. The woman's decaying hand grabbed my legs. The man pushed off the grate cover and hit her with a steel pole. The man lifted me out of the drain. The deformed man suddenly rouse up and grabbed the man helping me out of the drain. I had a choice, either help the man or slam the cover down. I slammed the cover down as the man screamed as the two pulled him under the water.

Bakers Farm

On the evening of October 12th 1984, a young couple drove down a long dirt road. The road seemed to go on for an eternity. As the couple drove past a little farm house on the left, they noticed a faint orange light coming from a window. A tree suddenly blocked the dirt road. The man driving the car turned sharply as the car turned over into a large field.

As the couple scrambled to set themselves free of the vehicle, a strange smell was in the air. The woman started to scream as she saw skeletons surrounding the vehicle. The man in the exited the car and was in shock to see skeletons surrounding him as they began to grab him. The screams from the man we're deafening as the skeletons pulled off his limbs and began to chant.

The woman exited the car and pushed her way past the skeletons as they began to pursue her down the dirt road. As the woman ran, she could see in the distance the orange glow from the farm house. As she ran, she noticed the skeletons gaining ground on her as she screamed, running toward the farm house. She made it to the front door as she yelled for help. The house owner opened the door and shouted, "Stay away from my house!" They promised not to harm us if we provide them with people to eat. The woman yelled as the skeletons grabbed her and disappeared into the night.

As the night became day, the only sign of the woman was a torn, bloody shoe by the farmhouse door. As the owner of the farm house exited their home, they began to bury the bloody shoe in the cold, dark earth. Later that day, the police showed up at the old farm house to question one of the owners. As the police cast a shadow on the old screen door to the farm house, an old woman said, how can I help you, officer? The officer stated they had found a crashed vehicle up the road and wondered if the old woman had seen anyone.

The old woman began to laugh. The old woman stated, as you already know officer, many strange things happen here. The old woman said she couldn't help the police. Suddenly, the officer smelled something strong. He asked if he could come inside. There was a loud bang. The old woman shot the officer, causing him to fall as he then realized what had happened. As she reached for him, he shot the old woman in the head, killing her instantly.

As he struggled to call for help, he heard something behind him. He quickly turned his head, he gasped as he could not believe what he was seeing. Skeletons surrounded him. They dragged him into the woods while he screamed. The old woman or the polices body were never recovered. As people drive past the old farm house, they say they still see the warm glow coming from the house.

Don't Tempt The Keeper Of The House

In the winter of 1982, a young man sees an ad in his local newspaper seeking a move in assistant. Gerald had just lost his job, and the ad seemed innocent enough. The next day, Gerald called the number to the ad and a woman answered the phone. At first, Gerald was surprised when he heard a voice that seemed to belong to a beautiful young woman. Oh! I am sorry, Gerald stated I must have the wrong number. I am calling an ad in the paper for a move – in assistant. Oh, this is the correct number my love, what is your name. My name is Gerald and what is yours, the voice seemed strained, just call me Vicky.

Vicky asked Gerald if he could come to the house to talk about the job. Gerald agreed that would be fine, what time should I arrive. Vicky stated she had some things to take care of first, she stated a later time would work better. Gerald said Vicky, a later time is ok for you? Vicky responded, Oh yes, I am a bit of a night owl as she began to laugh. Ok Vicky, what time is ok to arrive. Vicky stated 10:00pm is fine. Gerald agreed and said goodbye to the woman.

That evening, Gerald began to pack some bags for the journey. The address seemed a little further than Gerald had thought as he drove. Gerald drove for what seemed to be an eternity to reach the address. As he entered the property, he then drove to large wrought iron gates. As he exited his vehicle, he spotted something in the distance moving toward him.

It was difficult for Gerald to see through the fast approaching fog that laid at his feet like a thick blanket. Could you hear a voice in the distance? Are you here for Vicky? Gerald called out, yes, I am. Just as Gerald called, we could see an old, frail man approaching the interior of the large gate. Gerald noticed a small smile on the man's face as he unlocked the main gate.

As Gerald entered the home, he was in shock at how large the main area of the house was. The frail man asked Gerald to have a seat as he went to summon Vicky. Gerald looked around the house as, suddenly, he heard a door open at the top of the staircase. Gerald felt surprised. He saw a beautiful woman.

She looked at him while coming down the stairs. As the young woman approached Gerald, her smile was intoxicating as she sat close to him. Dear sir, I hope the drive was not too much for you. Oh, no, it was fine, stated Gerald as he could not stop staring at the woman's beauty. I have a question Vicky, why do you need a move – in assistant this place is spotless, what am I to do in this job? I require a strong young man to assist me with tasks around the manor.

When Vicky told Gerald how much she would pay him for his services, he could not say no as he stared at her beauty. As the man led Gerald to his room to stay the night, Gerald noticed the man smile strangely at the young woman. Gerald let go of the staircase rail as they started going up the stairs.

Suddenly, Gerald felt something on his hand. What is this as he yelled out. The older man looked at blood coming down Gerald's hand. Oh, dear sir, I apologize for serving you meat that was freshly killed today. I must have had blood on my hands as I came to the upper floors of the manor. I will take you to a washroom to clean your hands, my apologies, my dear sir.

As the old man led Gerald to a washroom to clean his hands, he heard the sound of a woman crying further down the hall. Sir, what is that sound? It sounds like someone crying down the hall. The old man said to Gerald, "Maybe you're tired from your long journey." Gerald agreed, "You're right, sir. Please take me to my room." This way sir, I will put you in the larger room tonight sir.

As Gerald followed the man to the large room, he noticed a small fire going in the fireplace. Gerald asked the old man what his name was, the old man who stated his name was Raymond. We'll thank you for all your help, Raymond. I am tired, and I am going to go to sleep now. Raymond replied it was good to have met you sir, have a good night. As Gerald walked a few steps toward the large bed and turned, Raymond was not in sight. I found it odd that Gerald thought I might be tired.

Gerald laid in bed and began to fall asleep, suddenly he heard the sound of a woman crying. He quietly walked to the door and listened for the sound. He slowly opened the door to the hallway. Furthermore, he then saw Vicky run by his room crying as Raymond followed her. Raymond, I can't do this to anymore to people. I have to stop. Vicky turned her head and looked at Gerald's room.

The door closed slowly. Vicky slowly walked to the rooms' door as Gerald looked through the keyhole in the door. Gerald forced his body against the door so no one could enter. He stood there for what seemed an eternity. Suddenly, Gerald felt something hit him on the side of his face. As he wiped his face with his hand, he saw it was crimson red blood. As he looked above him, he saw a hole in the ceiling as a horrible, disfigured creature was staring down at him. Blood seemed to be flowing out of its mouth.

Gerald ran and slid under the bed as Vicky and Raymond began to unlock the door to the room. As Vicky entered the room, she saw the window open. Raymond, he must have escaped through the window. Go look out in front of the house and find him. As Raymond exited the room, searching for Gerald.

Vicky began to walk out of the room as she suddenly turned and looked at the bed. Gerald tried to stop shaking as to not alert Vicky of his location. Vicky quickly reached down and grabbed Gerald by the leg as Gerald began to scream. Vicky yelled stop screaming Gerald, I am not going to harm you. I only want you to help me.

What do you want from me, Gerald screamed? I need you to live here with us for eternity. Gerald began to laugh loudly as Vicky's expression on her face changed quickly to anger. What are you laughing at Gerald, Vicky sarcastically stated. You foolish woman, nothing lives for eternity.

Raymond stares at Gerald, then touches his face and pulls the skin off while Gerald screams. Gerald, we are over two hundred years old, and you will be joining us one way or the other. Gerald pushed past Raymond and ran down the stairs and exited the manor. Raymond and Vicky ran, but suddenly stopped at the threshold of the doorway. What's wrong, screamed Gerald, I know the sunlight will kill you are vampires.

As Gerald turned his back to return to his car, he heard something behind him. As he turned, Vicky dove on top of him, quickly bitting into his neck. Vicky suddenly stood up and looked at Gerald as he was dying. You stupid man, we are not vampires. We are werewolves, the sunlight does not affect us.

Hallows Eve Trail

In the fall of 1978, a group of teens decided to venture down hallows eve trail. This dreadful decision would be their last. On October 31, 1978, Jim and his friend thought it would be fun to venture down hallows eve trail. The community warned the teens not to walk down the trail because others never came back. Jim invited his friend Adam to join, but first Adam was very reluctant to join in the trail walk. "Jim, are you crazy?" Adam asked with a deep voice. "You know what happened to others on this trail." They never returned.

Jim began to laugh, oh come on Adam what are you chicken. Adam said I am not afraid, it, just creepy to think about the story. We'll don't think about the story Adam and let's go tonight, it is October 31st. Adam reluctantly agreed to go with Jim. As the daylight faded into night, Jim showed up at Adam's house with a backpack and a small flashlight.

Adam left his room and quickly walked past his parents watching tv in the other room. As he exited his home, he asked Jim if he was sure he wanted to walk the train. Let's go, Adam, it will be fun. The boys saw a glimmer from the flashlight on the trail. They heard something behind them. The walk took longer than they thought. They arrived at a do not trespass sign on a fence. The fence was old and made of chain links. The two looked at each other with concern as they pushed open the fence.

As Jim flashed the light down the trail, he could see an old falling down house in the distance. As the two walked, they once again heard the sound of something moving behind them. The two boys began to run toward the old house to get away from whatever was behind them.

The two went into the old house and closed the door. They became quiet as they heard something approaching. Adam whispered Jim, can you see anything through the crack in the door? As Jim began to look through the door crack, he could see something walking in front of the house. Jim gasped what is it Jim, Adam frantically replied. Adam I don't know what it is, but it is not a person. Oh my god, Adam replied, what do you mean not a person? Adam, it is about nine feet tall and walks on two legs. Suddenly, the two boys started to scream as the creature let out a load roar.

Jim braced the door as he saw the creature look at the door and began to move quickly towards it. Jim screamed, Adam, help be hold the door shut, so it doesn't get in. As Adam pushes his hands firmly against the door to keep the creature out. The door shattered from the creature's power.

The two boys ran to another room and tried to flee through a window. The creature grabbed Jim as Adam fell through the window to the damp ground outside the old house. As the moonlights glow lit the face of Jim as the fierce creature was ripping him apart. Adam could hear the screams of Jim as Adam ran for his life. As the screams fell silent, Adam knew the creature had killed his friend, as it was probably chasing him now.

As, Adam could hear something running behind him as he ran. Suddenly, he slipped and fell to the ground. As he looked behind him, he could see the creature behind him walking slowly towards him. As Adam covered his eyes with his hands, the creature leaned down next to him and began to speak in a strange voice.

I will let you live this night if you will tell people to never walk the trail again and leave me in peace. Adam screamed, he would tell everyone not to walk the trail. Adam moved his hands from his face and saw the moonlight on the creature. The creature walked back to the old house. He quickly got up and started to run towards the old chain link fence. He opened the fence and ran towards home. Likewise, he looked back to check if the creature was chasing him.

Adam hurriedly went home and told his parents that something had caused Jim's death. He warned them not to go back to the trail and to let it remain undisturbed. That night, police arrived at Adams house and walked the trail to the old house. We found a bloody flashlight and some blood prints on the wooden floor of the house. The police left the trail to never return again.

The River Creature Of Bird River

As the warm summer month of July hit on the river's edge of Bird River, Md. So did the horrific tales about the River creature. Several years ago, a young teen decided it would be a challenge to swim to the channel marker. The distance did not seem too far for the teen, Kyle was a great swimmer. Two other boys told Kyle not to swim out that far due to the tale of the river creature. Oh! You can't be serious, guys, that is just something people say to keep us from swimming out too far.

Kyle looked down at the water and saw that not a ripple had formed; the surface of the water was truly like glass. Kyle stared at the water for a moment, then suddenly dove in. As he headed toward the channel marker, the two other boys watched.

Kyle started off at a slow pace as to conserve some of his energy for the swim back. Halfway to the marker, Kyle began to become afraid the marker was further than he had expected. Kyle heard the sound of something, but it was difficult to hear due to the water in his ears. As he turned toward his friends, he saw them frantically waving their arms at him. He then saw a trail of water movement coming his way fast.

Kyle turned and swam quickly toward the marker, as the trailing water was gaining speed on him. Kyle grabbed a deep breath and made it to the marker. As the water trail went past him, he could see something large under the water.

Oh! No, could the tale be true. Someone told him that the attacks on people happened at night. It was daylight outside. Did the tales tell about this creature? Was it hunting me now? The boys across the River stared at Kyle as he clung to the channel marker.

Kyle watched the creature go past him and go across the river to the other point. Kyle though if he could quickly get a head start on the creature, perhaps he could make it to the other side of the river.

He entered the water slowly, watching behind him. He moved through the water cautiously, hoping not to alarm the creature. Likewise, he thought if he could make it half way and conserve his energy, maybe he could outrun the creature to the other side. Kyle was at this point halfway across, there was no water movement towards him.

As Kyle focused his attention towards his friends, he heard a splash behind him. He quickly turned his head behind him as he swam toward the shoreline. The creature surfaced for a brief moment as Kyle drove his hands into the water for greater speed. As he got closer to the shore, the creature disappeared. This frightened Kyle even more, not having a visual of the creature.

Was it trying to circle in front of him to block his way to the shore. Kyle could hear his friends yelling for him to swim faster. Kyle grabbed another deep breath and gave it all he had. As he was close to the shore, the creature surfaced and its gigantic tail threw Kyle into a shoreline pier. Kyle's friends rushed to the pier to rescue him from the water. Despite their efforts, they could only partially lift him out. The boys yelled Kyle, what is wrong, we can get you out of the water. Suddenly, Kyle screamed as one of the boys saw something holding Kyle down in the water.

One of the boys ran to grab something to help get Kyle out with. As the boy quickly returned with a sharp pole to help release Kyle. The boys stabbed the flesh of the river creature in hopes of getting Kyle released from its grips. As Kyle was screaming, the boys saw it had him pinned to the pier.

As they stabbed one section of the creature, they then saw teeth down its appendages. It was moving the teeth back and forth, slowly cutting Kyle in half. The boys ran to get help. The men ran down to help Kyle. They could only see part of his torso. The creature quickly disappeared beneath the waves. We could not have done anything to save Kyle's life; sometimes stories are very true.

The Bloodlust Stranger

As the crisp fresh air descended from the tree line, the pure smell is unmistakable. I have lived here in Portland, Oregon for most of my life. The scenery is wonderful. I refer to it as pure life itself. All that changed in the fall of 2021. A strange new traveler came to join our quiet, peaceful community. At first, many locals ignored the strange man while watching his odd slanted walk. I had never seen anyone walk like he before.

I watched this man infiltrate the community. Weeks went by at first with no strange occurrences, then people started to disappear. Some locals seem to think maybe drowned or just moving away and not telling anyone. I suppose it is something darker than what is viewed.

On one brisk evening while walking my usual route. I saw the strange man walking in front of me walking up behind another person walking. His strange slanted walk turned into a slight run. The woman in front of me turned and saw the man approaching her from behind. I will never forget what happened next. The man sprinted to the woman and opened his mouth as he bit her throat out.

The look of terror on her face is forever etched in my memory. The creature turned back toward me as I hid behind a pine tree. The creature dragged the woman's body into the small patch of woods as I could not move, frozen with fear.

As I stand motionless, hearing the sounds of the creature devouring the woman's body. I saw the shadow of the creature walking up the path toward my location. Oh my God, I thought, does it know I am here!!! As I knew the creature was close to me, I dared not move. The sound of another person walking startled the creature. As its dull black face was in view, it fled.

I ran to the person walking and said to him, "Did you see the creature?" The man replied no I saw nothing sir, are you ok? I replied yes I am feeling tired sir. I walked away from the man as he stared at me walking away. Furthermore, I went home and called my Father, as he lived nearby. As the knock on my door startled me. My Father sat as I told him what I saw. He stated to me, he believes something like this happened long ago.

My Father became upset and said he would stay with me through the night. As darkness fell, a loud bang sounded from my rooftop. My Father ran upstairs to the upper floors of the house. As I entered the upstairs room, the creature was standing in front of my Father. The creature put out its large hands and pulled me into its chest. I am sorry son it has chosen you. There is nothing that I can do now. I screamed as the creature dragged me out the window. As I felt the bite of the creature deep into my neck. I could see my Father dropping to his knees.

The Modern Vampire of Baltimore

On January 10th of 2020, a series of horrific murders occurred in Baltimore, Maryland. The police couldn't find any leads. They only found the bodies, drained of blood.

The police questioned the locals about the crimes. The people said they saw a tall, slim man in black clothes near where the murders happened. One woman told police that she heard a loud scream but saw nothing.

Local police were patrolling on the evening of January 17th. As one police car turned into an alley, they spotted a tall, slender man wearing all black. He matched the description of the suspect. The police officer shined the spotlight on him as he stopped the police car. The officer yelled hey you stop, I want to talk to you. The tall, slender man ran off as he was being chased by the officer.

The thin man stopped running when the police officer approached. The officer noticed his long hands. The officer ordered the man to put his hands in the air and not to move. Suddenly, the slim man began to laugh as he said to the police officer, your weapons will not harm me, sir. The officer was shocked when he saw the slim man's pale face and glowing red eyes. The thin man raised his bloody hands and pointed at the police officer, saying, "Lower your gun and forget me." The man shot into the evening sky without a trace.

The officer walked back to his car, thinking about what had happened. He knew he couldn't talk about it. The next several days later there were no murders reported. A celebration event was to take place in the Baltimores Inner Harbor. The Harbor had many visitors the day of the event. People walked along the inner harbor and enjoyed the historic Ship the Constellation. They also went to the National Aquarium. The day seemed quiet and peaceful.

As the day turned into evening, Susan, a young woman, enjoyed the celebration near the inner harbor. As Susan was walking, she heard the sound of footsteps behind her. Susan turned and saw a tall, slender man wearing all black behind her. She began to feel frightened as she walked faster and faster to avoid the man.

As Susan rounded the corner of a building, she looked back and did not see the man who was following her. Susan took a deep breath and began to walk back to get to her car. She thought the man left and would not return. Susan walked slowly, checking for the slim man. She heard footsteps behind her. Looking back, she saw nothing. The slim man appeared. Susan realized he wasn't human. She ran to escape the creature. The creature darted after her. Susan knew she could not outrun this creature and stopped running.

Susan stopped running from the creature. The creature then walked toward Susan. As the creature began to get closer to Susan, she screamed out what are you and what do you want. The creature stopped and looked relatively startled by Susan's comments. Susan could now see the creature's face and long hands with extremely long nails. The creature started to walk more cautiously toward Susan.

Susan yelled, "I know what you are! You won't feast on me tonight!" As the creature lunged, she quickly reached into her overcoat. Susan fell to the ground, the vampire on top of her. Gasping, she watched as the wooden stake pierced his heart, turning him into ash. Susan got up and walked to her car.

The Winter Creatures Of The Woods

As snow starts to fall here in Maine, the sounds of the slight crackle against the glass is almost hypnotic. My name is Richard. I have lived here in Maine for the last twelve years. The process of moving due to the events that happened last year has been difficult. Likewise, I remember it vividly, going outside my cabin to get firewood for the fireplace. The deep snow was blinding as ice cycles hung from the cabin roofline. Walking to the woodpile, noticing footprints in the deep snow. The footprints were massive and not human, as I made my way quickly back to the cabin, something moved fast through the wood line. Grabbing my rifle and opened the door to take a shot. Suddenly something slammed against my house next to my head. A broken piece of firewood lay beside my feet. Staring into the white, blinding snow, I saw nothing at the wood line.

That night I did not sleep, hearing only a loud thump near the cabin. Grabbing my rifle and running to the back door, as I quickly turned on the spotlight, something ran into the woods. I shot my rifle into the air to scare it off. Likewise, seeing only a strange creature emerging from the wood line, raising my rifle for a shot, it disappeared into the thick snow-covered woods. Stunned by what was seen, I returned into my warm cabin and sat in my chair with my rifle next to me. No other events happened that night.

The next morning, I got dressed and ventured into the woods edge with my rifle in hand. The footprints away from my cabin are still visible in the deep snow. As I followed the prints farther and farther away from the cabin, I began to get chills. Suddenly, I saw in the distance a large snow-covered opening. As I neared the opening, a loud, strange sound resonates from it. As I began to run, I dropped my rifle into the deep snow, I didn't stop to retrieve my rifle. Fear resonated through me as I ran, occasionally looking behind me. As I saw my cabin in front of me, I heard something behind me approaching fast. Sprinting to the cabin's door, I stumbled with the keys as the creature emerged once again from the wood line. It slowly started to move forward toward me. As I entered my cabin and shut the door, the creature was almost to my back door.

As the day turned into night, my outdoor spotlights stayed on all night. Finishing my dinner from a chair, staring into the wood line. Suddenly, a loud crash, my windows glass flew all over the floor as I sat stunned at what I saw. My rifle was hanging in the broken window with large claw marks into the wood. Spotting the large creature run into the woods, I ran to another room to retrieve my shotgun and flashlight. Not only that, but I have had enough. Furthermore, I ran outside the cabin and into the woods. As I saw the creature running about 50 yards (ca. 46 m) from me, I raised my shotgun and took a shot, hearing the creature's loud screech as my shot struck it. As I began to aim at the fleeing creature for another shot. I then realized the creature slowed down in front of me and fell to the ground. As I began to approach the creature for a final shot, the strange feeling as if someone or something were watching come over me. Hearing a loud growl behind me, as I slowly turned, the woods behind me was full of large creatures just like the one that lay in front of me.

The group of creatures behind me began to scream loudly. Frozen with fear, raising my shotgun, not knowing what would happen next. One creature darted quickly toward me as I shot it. The creature dropped in front of me as blood pooled out beside it. The creatures ran at me as I tried to get another shot. All I remember is being slashed and bitten as I fell into the deep snow. Faintly hearing a loud shot as I lost consciousness. I awoke in the hospital. A strange man leaning over me. Hi there, my name is Drew. I am glad I got to you in time, the creatures fled as I approached you. Never again have I encountered the creatures. I forever hear the loud screams of the creatures in my head.

The Darkness Among The Reeds

As a child, I vividly remember running to the reeds with my younger brother Richard. One late evening, Richard wanted to venture into the reeds. The thought of that chilled me to the bone, Richard ran out the back door and down toward the reeds, as he ran I suddenly spotted movement in the tree line.

I screamed for my brother to stop, but his laughter drowned out my screams. I began to run to catch him as I started to gain ground. Suddenly, I was knocked to the ground by something passing me from behind. I lay in a small ditch as Richard's screams, muffled slightly. As I try to scream out, I have no sound, only the silent air coming from my mouth. The creature carried my brother into the night.

To this day, Richard has never been seen again. I still venture to the reeds. I will not say I am not afraid, but the lure of seeing my brother proceeds the fear of such a creature. Likewise, I will forever search for my brother.

The sound of the reeds sifting through to me leaves me terrified and curious at the same time, as I stand and wait for it to descend upon me, the anticipation of its arrival leaves me motionless. The smell that emanates from the reeds is hypnotic, the earthy undertones and the scent of decaying matter is beyond our imagination.

I have journeyed to this place since I was young, trying to get a glimpse of it as it slowly approaches me from behind, as I turn it disappears into the night. You cannot understand its allure until you are frozen with fear. The suspense of not knowing if it will launch an attack as I stand motionless. I know the scent of death permeates around me from all directions, as I stand waiting to get one glimpse of it. I do not know what it is and nor do I care.

Likewise, I am addicted to the fear of not knowing what it is, I suppose if I knew what it was the thrill would be gone. Some people think I am crazy to search out such a creature. I almost think it is aware of the fear I am extracting from its arrival. As time goes on, it gets closer to me as I fill my addiction of fear. Perhaps it gets some kind of thrill of instilling the fear in me as well.

I will always come to this place at night, until the day it no longer arrives to fill my appetite of true fear. I know when it is near, waiting to fill my needs once again with the darkness among the reeds.

One early June morning, I ventured into the reeds, searching for the creature that had taken my brother. I loaded a backpack with a flashlight and a camera. My hopes of at least getting a photo of this creature propelled me to the last area Richard was spotted. As the daylight was lost tonight, I began to hear movement around me. As I reached for my camera, I saw the large creature standing before me, it's arms covered with dark hair. What kind of beast was this?? As I quickly snapped a photo, the light from the flash enraged the creature. The camera suddenly dropped from my hand. I did not feel the pain until the camera's flash went off as it hit the ground. One split second glimpse of my severed arm lay next to me as the only thing I remember is the crimson red contrast of my blood on the camera.h I suppose I will be a forever part of The Darkness Of The Reeds.

The Groves

As the cool night air covers me as I walk through the groves, I am not alone. The scent of strong decay permeates the air as I walk, I dare not turn around. I hear the sounds of slight gargles, is it human or some demon coming to claim my soul. As I slowly turned my eyes to meet its eyes staring into mine, my breathing became shallow as I was paralyzed with fear. It's soft voice said don't struggle, James it is much easier this way. The creature told me it would spare my life only if I would bring more people to him to feast upon. As I looked to the ground, the sight of bloody body parts scattered on the surrounding ground. I screamed at the demon as it opened its mouth. I screamed, I will do it!!! Likewise, I will bring you people if you spare me this night.

Furthermore, I broke the demon's grip and ran to my house. Besides, I stayed in the house for days on end, hoping the demon would forget about the promise I had made it. After the third night, I saw the demon fly to the rooftop. I could hear the chilling voice speak out, James, I am waiting for you to bring people to the groves. I screamed out, leave me this night, I need time to do as you ask. The demon said I will give you ten days, as the tenth day arrives I will come for your soul, James.

The days came and went with no sight of the demon. James began to try to devise a plan to stop the demon from taking another soul. As the ninth night came, James had his plan in place. The tenth night came the demon flew to the rooftop and the soft voice became loud, James your time is up, you did not do as I had asked. I will dine on your soul this night.

The demon shouted come to the groves, or I will come in and get you, if you come to the groves I will end your life quickly. If I have to break in to get you, I will feast on you slowly. James shouted demon I will come to the groves. The sight of the demon flying into the groves chilled me to the bone, but my plan had to stop it. I slowly began to walk to the groves to meet my end. As I walk, I see the demon standing waiting for me. Suddenly, the demon grabs me as its teeth sever my limbs to the bone. I did not scream but began to laugh out load. As the demon released me, I yelled out, I ingested poison before you began to feast on me. Now you will never again feast on another. As my sight began to blur, the demon fell to the ground next to me.

The Blood-Red Alaskan Stream

The harsh winters in Alaska bring more than below 0 temps and dangerous wildlife. My name is Greg and I have lived here since I was a young boy. I will share my terrifying story with you. When I went for a hike through the dense woods leading up a steep hillside. I heard a load strange noise I have never heard before. As I unclenched my partiality frozen fingers around the trigger on my rifle, I saw something knocking down trees and brush In front of me. I gasped as I saw a large seemingly human like creature coming straight at me. I braced myself as the creature darted toward me, I raised my rifle quickly and shot, a loud boom sounded out as the creature let out a strange roar. As it passed, I will forever remember seeing its eyes fixed with mine as it past me, quickly knocking me to the ground.

As I slowly open my eyes laying partially down a small hill. The creature must have struck me with immense force. I had been cut up somewhat but could still slowly stand as I scanned the blinding snow to assure the creature was gone. I grabbed a stiff branch and walked slowly as I retrieved my rifle laying next to me in the deep snow. Likewise, I finally saw my cabin at the top of the hill, occasionally looking back to make sure the creature was not coming up behind me. As I walked, the deep snow was crimson, stained by blood. I thought I had been injured, the blood belonged to the creature that fled. I was too weak to follow the injured creature. Likewise, I reached the cabin and locked the door tightly, as I also barricaded the entrance to my cabin to assure the creature would not come for me to get its revenge for injuring it.

Furthermore, I stayed awake all night as I heard load roars seemingly coming deep from the woods. My rifle stayed by my side the entire night. The next morning as the roars became louder.

I saw movement from multiple places deep into the woods. The first large creature emerged facing the cabin as it roared loudly. As the creature starting moving toward my cabin, I loaded my 44 magnum handgun and grabbed my rifle. I walked to the cabins' door as two other creatures came from the left side of the woods. I gasped as the two creatures were dragging the creature I shot as they screamed loudly. As I raised my rifle to take a shoot at the creature closer to me, I heard something behind me, as I turned, my front door was standing open.

Suddenly, a creature grabbed me and through me to the ground outside the cabin. As I lay stunned by slamming onto the ground. The creatures surrounded me, roaring so loud I could feel it. The creatures drop something on top of me as they screamed. I closed my eyes to prepare for my end. As I lay in the freezing snow, the silence was deafening, was I dead?? I slowly opened my eyes and the creatures were gone. I began to stand as I saw a small dead creature next to me. The small creature was coated with long white hair, large eyes and hands and feet similar to my own. As I touched the small creature I saw bullet wounds on its side matching the size of my rifle. Oh! no was the creature I saw in the deep woods carrying the small creature that I shot. I started to stand grasping the small creature in my hands. The sadness I experienced at that point was overwhelming, as I looked toward the wood line, the sight of the large creatures staring at me through the wood line chilled me to the bone!

I walked toward the creatures and laid the small creature at the edge of the woods, it seemed like the thing to do at the time. As I slowly walked toward the cabin, the creatures once again emerged from the woods and grasped the small creature and slowly walked into the woods while looking back in my direction. I have never seen the creatures again. I will never search for these creatures again and leave them in peace.

The Haunting Of Briggs Hotel

On August 12, 1998, a young woman decided to venture to the historic Briggs Hotel. The hotel was built in the 1800s and had a horrific tragedy. Ann lived in New York and always wanted to stay at the Briggs Hotel for a few nights, despite being aware of the events that occurred there long ago.

As Ann drove on the curved drive leading to the large entrance, she suddenly felt a strange chill cover her like a blanket. She saw a tall man waiting at the door, staring at her from a distance. As she slowly walked to the entrance, the tall man asked if he could help her. Hi, my name is Ann and I have a reservation. The man slowly looked up and had a strange smile on his face. As I walked past him inside the hotel, I began to smell a putrid smell emanate from another room. I quickly turned, and the man was gone.

I grasped my bag and began to ascend the staircase to the upper level of the hotel. As I walked, the dimly lit hall.

I suddenly stoped as a dark figure formed in front of me. I stood motionless as the figure raised a hand. The loud sound of something falling hitting the hardwood floor will stay with me forever. The dark figure disappeared in front of my eyes. The slight glimmer of an object laying on the floor was horrifying and exciting at the same time. I walked toward the object on the floor as I gasped. It was a slightly worn skeleton key.

As daylight turned to night, I started to search the hotel to find the door the key would open. I began to hear a child weeping. An apparition of a small girl walked out of an adjacent room. As the child walked close to me, I quickly shut my eyes with the hope it was only in my mind. As I opened my eyes, the child walked through me, rendering me motionless and short of breath as I fell to the floor. When I awoke, I was laying in bed in a large room with the door slightly shut. How did I get here ?? I can't remember walking inside the room.

I slowly got out of bed and made my way to the door. Likewise, I paused as I began to hear people talking lightly. I opened the door and no one was there?? I saw the large staircase and started to descend the stairs as the dark figure once again appeared in front of me and pointed toward the large front doors. Furthermore, I quickly ran down the stairs and toward the door as I saw apparitions forming on the staircase. My car was in sight as I fled the hotel. As I sped away, looking back, the image of the child standing in the doorway will be forever etched in my memory.